BUGGING OUT

The Bugging Out Series: Book One

NOAH MANN

Published By Schmuck & Underwood

ISBN-10: 1499502494
ISBN-13: 978-1499502497

Those who expect to reap the blessings of freedom must, like men, undergo the fatigue of supporting it.

Thomas Paine

Part One

The Blight

One

Just south of Arlee, at the checkpoint on Route 93, I watched two soldiers from the Montana National Guard shoot a man who refused to disarm after stepping from his ten-year-old pickup.

I saw it from three cars back, my window rolled down, enough of the exchange drifting past the idling engines ahead that it was clear the man, who looked about fifty and was as anonymous to me as his killers, had reached some tipping point. One too many roadblocks, it might have been, having to exit his vehicle and have his shoes checked for spores, his tires sprayed down with chemicals the public had been assured were harmless to all but the invasive blight the concoction was designed to eradicate. Or one too many times having to surrender his sidearm, worn open instead of concealed, a practice that was either a longstanding preference of the man, or a statement of defiance.

He could just as easily have kept his weapon concealed beneath a coat or untucked shirt, as mine was while the incident unfolded, and the part-time soldiers would have never exerted the authority they'd been granted to 'Temporarily Disarm Travelers of Visible Weapons' while operating the checkpoint. The edict had come down from some federal bureaucracy with exactly that wording, and was stated explicitly on signage visible as one approached any one of the dozen checkpoints I'd passed through in the west of Montana, sometimes on a daily basis. Checkpoints that dotted the whole of the nation now like way stations where freedoms the populace had taken for granted were suspended. Most surrendered their rights willingly in the belief they did so for some greater good.

The man near Arlee was no longer one of those people.

He became the immovable object standing against the unstoppable force, a collision that ended with the FDA agent supervising the checkpoint screaming at the Guardsmen to 'secure the troublemaker'.

Secure the troublemaker...

They moved toward him, he reached for his pistol, rifle shots cracked sharp, and the man went down. Drivers in their cars ducked down, terrified. I didn't. I should have, but I didn't. I couldn't. The event held me rapt. Playing out like some slow motion human tragedy, lifeblood spilling from the man and puddling on the dirty shoulder of the road beneath the endless blue summer sky.

It was terrible enough to witness that, but what happened next cemented the belief I held, one that had been building over the past several weeks, that things had fundamentally changed. The benign distrust and disgust that had been simmering between citizen and government for more than a decade now manifested itself as something not external to the power structure, but *within* it. The organs of the state were rotting from the inside. I knew this for certain when one of the Guardsmen, after standing over the body of the man he'd shot, turned to face the FDA official and leveled his rifle at the incredulous man, eyeing him with withering contempt before emptying what remained in his magazine into him. The functionary from Washington spun and crumpled onto the hot asphalt as other Guardsmen rushed their comrade, taking him to ground in what looked a rugby scrum decked in woodland camouflage.

Screams rose. The killer Guardsman broke free of the attempt to subdue him, abandoning his empty rifle and drawing his sidearm. He chambered a round and waved the pistol at his fellow Guardsmen. Young men who were most likely friends. Possibly even close friends. They held back and tried to talk him out of his weapon as a National Guard lieutenant raced toward the scene from the checkpoint's command post some hundred yards up the road.

The killer Guardsman, who news reports would later identify as twenty-four year old Kyle Ames of Bozeman, saw his superior rushing his way, drawing his own sidearm, screaming at the young man to drop his weapon. But he didn't. In an act that might have been the most honorable thing I witnessed while stopped at that checkpoint, Kyle Ames raised his pistol and put it under his chin and pulled the trigger.

The maelstrom of screams that began with the first volley of shots spun loud and desperate now, from cars where travelers huddled in fear, and from uniformed young men and women paralyzed by what they'd just witnessed. Orders were shouted. Radio calls went out. It was chaos.

But in my pickup, some sense of calm filled me. I didn't know how to explain it right then, but in the days and weeks that followed I was able to think back to that moment and began to realize that I'd been, oddly, fortunate to witness what I had. In an instant, there, on that lonely stretch of highway, my eyes were opened to accept what was going to come. Had I not seen that, up close, without the filter of a television screen and talking head journalist between myself and the truth, I might never have believed what an old friend, my oldest friend, was going to tell me after summer turned to fall.

Two

My foreman stood with me in my office and stared at the TV mounted to the wall, the both of us quietly incredulous at the images being broadcast, the same on every channel, talking heads trying to give context to what the audience was seeing. None was needed. What had happened was as plain as day. The amateur video told the story.

"Can you believe this?" Marco asked, expecting no answer. "This is insane."

The truth was, I could believe it. It had been two months since the shooting at Arlee. There'd been other incidents around the nation, if reports sneaking past official attempts to quash them were accurate. There were no reasons to think they weren't. Especially for me. I'd seen it happen.

And now it was happening again. On a larger scale.

"How could they do that?" Marco asked. The question, this time, seemed directed to some higher power. One that might, in some infinite wisdom, be able to explain, if not justify, what we were seeing.

And what we were seeing was clear. Horrific and clear. Recorded from an Arizona highway by a motorist stopped to document a glorious sunset on his phone's camera, the twenty second video began with two bright spots against the darkening sky, one small, one large, both moving fast and low. Aircraft, it was clear, the larger one seeming to be leading the smaller one. Or, what it was in actuality, the smaller one chasing the larger one.

Hunting it.

An exclamation from the man recording the incident preceded a stream of hot white specks spewing from the smaller aircraft. Then a curse from him as he realized that he was watching cannon fire from an Air Force fighter slice into a passenger jet, sending the larger plane into a wobbling descent as a wing sheared off, trailing fire, the whole of the fuselage disappearing behind a hill where a fireball bubbled skyward just before the sickly crack of an explosion reached the cameraman.

Every station was playing the footage detailing the final seconds of Flight 82. The final seconds of the one hundred and ninety souls aboard. People who had been trapped on the wrong side of the southern border when it was closed a week earlier. American citizens just wanting to get home to their families. Unrest spreading north from Central America had forced them into a desperate act, with the full cooperation of the flight crew. The story being reported indicated that the veteran pilots had filed a flight plan from Mexico City to Jamaica, but shortly after takeoff deviated from that and flew north toward the United States. Radio communications with the plane revealed that neither pilots nor passengers believed they would face any serious resistance to their return.

They were wrong.

"This is all kinds of crazy," Marco commented, shaking his head, as angry as I'd ever seen him. The kind of anger that couldn't be directed at any one thing, or person.

Things had gotten worse. Worse than checkpoints where citizens were shot down for doing nothing more than going about their daily lives. Now they were being shot out of the sky. Terrorists could fly jets into buildings, but Americans who just wanted to come home were dropped like some sort of enemy invaders.

Marco was right to be incredulous at everything. The checkpoints. The federal raids on warehouses holding 'unapproved imports'. Corn chips and cereal, for God's sake. They were sending in SWAT teams to confiscate snacks and breakfast foods simply because a single ingredient in them had come from a country where the blight had *later* set in.

It was hard to believe this had all started almost a year ago in a potato field in Poland, a hundred miles from the capital, Warsaw, when a farmer saw a spot on a leaf. A small patch of grey that might have been a gathering of dust clinging to morning dew.

But it wasn't.

The farmer had first noticed the blemish when it was no larger than the tip of his thumb. He paid it no great attention, and only recalled that he'd seen it at all a week later when his entire crop, nearly a hundred acres, was little more than a wilting landscape of grey death, rotting and reeking. Local officials from the Ministry of Agriculture and Rural Development examined the field, took samples, but could offer no explanations to the farmer as to why a field that had been in his family for nearly two hundred years seemed suddenly afflicted with some terrible disease. They promised to look into it further, but had little more they could offer him beyond sympathy and vague assurances.

One of the visiting officials left the site and traveled thirty miles to his next appointment. A routine stop at another farm where cabbage grew as far as the eye could see. He was there to deliver an inspection report to the farmer approving his use of a new automated bundling and baling system. He'd known the man for several years and on this visit spent an hour talking with him as they strolled between the rows of bright green cabbage, microscopic spores shedding from the official's boots with each step he took.

A week later not a head of cabbage was left viable on the farm. Ten days after that, not a single crop of any foodstuff within 100 miles was anything more than a pile of noxious organic waste. Government functionaries from Poland, Belarus, Ukraine, and Lithuania struggled to understand the relentless disease spreading across their lands. They tallied the damage in lost product and increased cost of imported food for their population. But, to a person, every single brain the affected governments were throwing at the problem insisted the agricultural malady could, and would, be alleviated.

Then the pine trees began dying.

The story of how the blight had been discovered, and how it had spread in less than a year across Europe and Asia, finally arriving in South America, had been blasted across news outlets with the urgency of some approaching asteroid. One savvy network had even branded the unknown disease 'The Blight' in a stroke of marketing genius. And, with every story that told of the consequences a worldwide spread of the affliction would bring, equally vehement reassurances came from governments near and far. The United States, in particular, provided expert upon expert to detail the steps being taken to contain, identify, and, eventually, eradicate the blight.

But experts had no sway over the effects already being felt. Food prices had skyrocketed. And not just things that grew in the ground or on trees. The steaks people loved to hear and smell sizzling on their grills had legs before slaughter, and wandered fields chewing on grasses that, in many countries, were now dead or dying. Beef, chicken, pork—all depended in some form on plant life to survive and thrive. In countries where the blight had struck, creatures, be they domesticated for food or wild for hunting, were dying.

Maybe, though, the worst byproduct of the blight was fear. Fear that was edging toward panic. Governments were shooting their own citizens out of dazzling skies, and individuals, too, were taking extreme measures. Farmers across the nation's grain belt stood guard 24/7 to keep anyone from approaching their fields, despite leaked word that the primary way the blight's infectious spores were transmitted was on the feet of birds. All it would take was a flock of geese sunning themselves in some dying field in Brazil and then winging north to Canada, stopping along the way to eat, rest, and spread the death before continuing on their migration.

"I don't see a good ending to all this," Marco said.

"Neither do I," I said, the image of the crash's fireball bright on the screen.

The phone on my desk buzzed. I snatched it up and stayed focused on the television. "Yeah?"

"There's a man here to see you," my assistant, Marjorie, said.

"Do I have an appointment I forgot?"

"No."

"Who is it?"

For just an instant she hesitated. "He didn't say. I mean...he *wouldn't* say."

I took the remote in hand and muted the TV. "Okay. Send him in."

"That's another odd thing," Marjorie said. "He said for you to meet him out front. He didn't want to wait inside."

"Okay. I'll be out in a minute." I hung up and looked again to the TV screen, Marco shaking his head as the fireball rose against a darkening sky, lives ended in high-definition.

"Christ," he said in a soft exclamation.

"Yeah," was all I could say as I headed out.

* * *

Son of a bitch...

That was my first reaction when I saw the man pacing on the sidewalk in front of my building. I gave it voice with a slight degree less coarseness.

"I'll be damned."

Neil Moore heard my voice and turned.

"How are you, Fletch?" he asked, choosing, as he had for the past two decades, the truncated nick over my given name. I doubted he'd ever spoken the words *Eric Fletcher* since I'd know him.

"I thought you were dead," I said. It had been six months since I'd heard a peep from him. "Or worse."

Neil snickered, the expression of humor light and tired, some effort seeming necessary to manage it. "What's worse than dead?"

"I'd say D.C., but you've been there."

It had been a point of joking contention between us, our friendship stretching back some twenty years to days charging tackling dummies at U.S. Grant High while Coach Macklin screamed at us. There we'd learned to hit hard, and to take a hit. We also learned how to play hard. And, most importantly, to work hard. Each of us had done just that, me skipping the books and frat parties to build a contracting business from the ground up, while Neil aced two degrees at college and bulled his way through department bureaucracy to a position of near-importance at the State Department.

"What are you doing back in Missoula?"

He thought for a moment, as if searching for the right answer. Or any answer at all. In the end he skipped replying altogether and posed his own question.

"You got a few minutes you can spare for me?"

It was an absurd question, I knew. I would always make time for Neil. Still, it was nearly as absurd that my friend would show up unannounced. A simple phone call prior to his arriving would have allowed plans to be made, as we had during past visits to the city we grew up in.

"You know I do," I said, sensing something in the silence that followed. Something beyond hesitation. "Neil, is everything all right?"

"Remember the burger place where you spilled your shake on Mary?"

Mary Derek. I hadn't thought of her in over a dozen years. Neil had been there, and had seen the apoplectic mess that Mary became when the cup of soupy vanilla tipped over on her lap. He knew the name of the Burger place—Astro Burgers—but didn't say it. He was being cryptic. Intentionally, it seemed.

"Yeah," I said. Behind me, gravel trucks rolled past on their way to a construction site.

Neil looked up the street in one direction, then the other, before fixing his gaze upon me. A wariness swirled about him. Something that wasn't quite fear. But wasn't far from it, either.

"Meet me there as soon as you can," Neil said, then turned and walked quickly up the block, turning the corner without as much as glance back in my direction.

* * *

Neil was waiting, sitting at one of the outside tables, ignoring the season, his jacket zipped to his neck. He stood when I stepped from my pickup truck in the adjacent parking lot and approached.

"I'm sorry about the evasiveness back there," he said to me, then pulled me into a bro hug and thumped my back before easing away. "It really is good to see you."

The statement felt truer than anything I'd heard him say. Ever.

"Yeah," I told him, sharing the sentiment. "Neil, what's going on?"

He sat at the table and I slid onto the bench across from him. He'd ordered a cup of coffee from the takeout window before I arrived and now wrapped his hands around it, staring at the wisp of steam swirling upward from the drink.

"I'm going to tell you something, Eric, and then I'm going to leave, and you'll never see me again."

It took me a second to process what he'd just said. To absorb the utter impossibility of the statement. My head cocked a bit to one side and I actually smiled, because this had to be some joke, or the prelude to one.

But it was not. Even before he uttered a single word of explanation, the air of solemnity hung thick around him. When he looked up from his coffee and met my gaze, there was dread in his eyes.

"Neil, what the hell..."

"You still keeping up that property north of Whitefish?"

"Yeah," I confirmed to him. My two hundred acre slice of heaven. The serviceable house that sat on it now dated from the 1930s, but I had plans to demolish it and the barn and old outbuildings to put up my dream retreat. The place I would retire to and spend my best days.

"How far are you there from the main road? Not the highway, but that road splits off from it?"

I had to do some mental math, and recall the survey reports from ten years ago when I purchased the land. Possibly I should have wondered why he was asking such a thing. He was my friend, and something, whatever it was, had brought him here. Something had raised the importance of seemingly mundane facts for him.

"From Weiland Road there's a gravel driveway about two hundred yards," I told him. He'd been there before on several occasions, mostly to relax, fish in the pond on the property, and send some bullets downrange in the area I'd set aside for shooting. He'd still never joined me for a deer hunt, using the house there as our own private lodge, but I had hope that he still would. Someday.

He thought on what I'd told him and leaned over the table a bit, narrowing the distance between us. His gaze shifted left, then right, as if clearing the area before proceeding.

"Neil, you're kinda spooking me," I said. There was a hint of levity in my delivery. Some attempt to lighten, or brighten, his mood.

It didn't work.

"You've been following this crop disaster in Europe?"

"It's kinda hard to ignore," I said, recounting for him what I'd witnessed near Arlee. The tentacles of the blight sweeping across Europe had reached our shores in ways more sinister than just higher priced steaks and vegetables. That was my opinion, at least.

"It's going to get worse," he said to me.

"I get that feeling, too. People will gladly submit for inspection by soldiers, but they cry bloody murder when the price of their porterhouse goes through the roof."

"They haven't seen anything yet," Neil said, some gravity about him. A darkness like I'd never known him to exhibit. "None of us have."

"What are you talking about?"

"You need to start paying attention, Fletch."

"To what?"

"Watch everything you can. Read everything you can. What you're hearing now is what they want you to hear. The governments over there, our government here, they're saying the situation is being managed." Neil eased back a bit and chuckled lightly, no humor in the expression at all. Just comical disdain. "Managed."

What he'd said to me sounded more than vaguely like a warning. But a warning of what?

"Okay," I told him. "I'll keep tabs on it. But what does any of this have to do with my property?"

"How are you stocked there? Water, consumables, food? Not the perishable crap, but stable supplies. Things that will last. Things that will sustain you."

I saw suddenly where he was going with this, and it reminded me why we'd meshed so easily back in our younger days. We thought alike in many respects. Appraised the world and the ways of its various institutions similarly. We trusted ourselves, and expected others to earn the same. Be they individuals, or those elected to lead.

"I started stocking up a while back," I told him. "After that insanity up near Arlee, I knew things were going to hit a boiling point sooner or later."

"Sooner," Neil told me. "Sooner."

I nodded. I'd suspected as much.

"I laid in enough for a few months, just in case," I explained. "MREs, barrels for water. I made sure the batteries for the solar system were good to go. And I picked up ammo. Lots of ammo. If things get dicey, I'll be able to ride it out up there."

For a moment he said nothing. Gave no reaction. No nod of approval, or '*good thinking*'. He just looked at me, silent, as if he didn't want to tell me what he knew he'd have to.

"You're not ready."

I let his observation hang for a moment between us, wondering how he could so openly state such a thing. Then, that which should have worried me became apparent—what did he know that made him offer such an appraisal?

"Neil, what the hell is going on?

"You need to think in terms of years, Fletch. Not months."

"Years?"

He nodded. "Two or more."

"Years?" I pressed him, struggling to grasp what he was suggesting, or the reason behind it. "*Two* years?"

"At least."

It had to be plain on my face, that I wasn't fully processing what he was telling me.

"This isn't some storm you're going to just casually avoid by an extended stay at your getaway. Not just a few knuckleheads rioting until order is reestablished."

"Okay. Then what the hell *is* coming? You seem to be tiptoeing around it, whatever it is you're trying to share with me."

This was the thing that worried me the most. We'd never been bullshitters, especially with each other. And we'd never pulled our punches, physically or otherwise. We knew each other could handle whatever needed to be done, or said.

"It's all tumbling down," he said, almost matter-of-factly.

"What do you mean 'all'?"

His gaze swelled a bit. "All. Everything. Government, countries, economies, societies."

It was my turn to lean forward. My stare narrowed down on my friend. The empty space around us outside the restaurant seemed suddenly claustrophobic. As if everyone inside was also leaning in for a listen.

"What do you know, Neil?"

"Six weeks ago I'm attached as a liaison from State to a team going down to Brazil."

"What kind of team?"

He hesitated for just a moment as a car cruised slowly by, then turned at the nearby corner, disappearing around it.

"A joint mission from Department of Agriculture and USAMRIID."

The glazed-over look I gave him at the acronym prompted some clarification.

"United States Army Medical Research Institute for Infectious Diseases."

The expansion of the letter jumble into real world terms didn't completely wipe the fog from my comprehension.

"Agriculture and Army disease specialists?"

"Yes."

"I was the go-between for them and the Brazilians."

"Okay..."

Maybe Neil was waiting for me to come to an understanding myself. To piece together what he'd shared. But I was still drawing a blank.

"It's bad there, Fletch. Brazil has a huge agricultural industry, and the blight is spreading like wildfire."

A sick warmth stirred in my gut. Word that the blight had crossed an ocean wasn't new, though it took the involved governments weeks to admit as much after an equal amount of time issuing stern denials.

"Plant geneticists from Ag were there to verify the strain," he said. "Same as Poland. No mutation. The thing is a monster."

"All right. That explains one side of your team. Why the hell was the Army tagging along?"

"Because the blight is behaving like a disease," Neil explained. "That's what I picked up from the discussions they were having. I wasn't supposed to know any of this, but... Fletch, it's moving through vegetation like the plague rolling over a population."

"Wait...are you saying this is like some weapon?"

He shook his head.

"No. No one knows, really. Nature is fully capable of screwing us over if conditions are right. And here it looks like conditions were just right for this to begin. First in Poland, and then all it took were a few spores from a contaminated crop to hitch a ride on a plane, or boat, and what was something isolated to Europe and Asia is now a continent hopper."

"How widespread is it in Asia?" I pressed him.

"Russia, into China, Vietnam. Some of those places haven't become part of the wider conversation yet, but they will be. Soon."

I sat back, leaning away from the table. The gravity Neil had brought with him had now infected me. A realization rose as to the timing of this get together we were having.

"It's here," I said. "Isn't it?"

Neil took a stuttered breath and nodded.

"In a cranberry bog, of all places. In Oregon. And if it's there, it's going to be everywhere."

"Okay," I said, my head spinning, but still trying to grasp the totality of the situation. "So it kills some crops—"

"No." Neil shook his head. "Not some...*all*. Everything. It kills every single plant it comes in contact with. Not just crops. Trees, bushes, even damn weeds. And when the plants die, the animals aren't far behind."

"And the recovery time?" I asked, fearing what the answer would be.

"The Ag scientists were scared. One of them made it pretty clear he didn't see any sort of recovery."

We sat there in silence for a moment, staring at each other, me absorbing all that Neil had shared, and him waiting, just waiting, to let me process the same.

"It all comes tumbling down," I said, recounting his earlier statement. "I understand what you meant now."

"You can tell people there's a shortage of rubber so they can't have tires for their car. Or heating oil, so they're going to have to throw extra logs on the fire instead of run the furnace. But you can't tell them they're going to go hungry. You can't tell them they're going to watch their children starve. No government has the guts to tell that truth. There's a dam of denial built around what's happening and it's going to burst. When it does..."

It was part sermon, part indictment. And it was scaring the hell out of me.

"How is it possible that this isn't news already?" I wondered aloud. "I mean, it's not as sexy as a meteor hitting the earth, but the aftermath won't be too different."

"There are rumblings," he told me. "I'm not the only one asking questions. Agencies are starting to lock down information. Even things that have nothing to do with this. They're just getting ready for when everything *does* have to do with this. There's enormous pressure on news agencies right now to hold damning stories."

"But the shoot down..."

"That's a gimme," Neil said. "The power structure would rather have the population fixated on a horror like that than the real shit coming down the drain at everyone."

This was as far from what I'd anticipated we'd talk about as anything could be. I'd expected some generally friendly jawing with my friend. Thought we might inhale some burgers and share a plate of onion rings. Not talk about the end of everything we'd come to know.

"Fletch," Neil began, sliding the now chilled cup of coffee aside as he leaned on the table, "you have to get ready now. Really ready. This is all going to leak. It could be ten days, or ten hours, but the rumblings are going to become a roar, and when that happens it will be too late to prepare."

"My getaway," I said, that thread connected now. "You think we should head up there."

I didn't expect what Neil did next—he shook his head.

"You," he corrected. "You have no encumbrance. No wife, no girlfriend, unless things have changed. Your parents are gone. No brothers or sisters. All you have to leave behind is a building, a bunch of trucks, and people who are good and dead no matter what you do."

"Neil..."

He smiled, and it seemed to me that he'd accepted some fate rolling toward him in slow-motion.

"I can't leave my father," Neil said.

His father—one hell of a man who I'd spent nearly as much time with as my own dad while growing up. Dieter Moore, or as I'd called him on every occasion we've been together, *Mr.* Moore. Once he'd been a tank of a man. Strong, self-reliant. He'd give you a hand up, but not a handout. And now...now he sat wasting in a nursing home recliner, cancer chewing away at what was left of his insides. A year ago the doctors had given him six months to live, but the stubborn old man was flipping their educated approximations the bird by hanging on. Neil, I knew, could no more abandon his father and run for the hills with me than I could mine if he was still alive.

"Damn, Neil."

"Right now, Fletch, you have to stop thinking about me. About anything. You have to look past any distractions. While everyone else is still thinking the limit of this is paying more in the checkout line at the grocery store, you have to get ready. Before they get wise."

But how the hell did someone get ready for this? This wasn't running to the store to stock up on canned goods because a blizzard was coming. If what Neil was predicting was true, the Almighty might as well drop a rock from space on the planet and end everything quickly.

"Hey," Neil said sharply. "What are you doing?"

He'd caught me. Mentally going to a dark place where giving up was an option.

"What did Macklin always yell at us?" Neil asked. "When we were beat down, by him, the other team, whatever? You remember what he'd scream at us?"

I did. No way I could ever forget the words of that lovely bastard.

"Life's tough. Be tougher."

He nodded, a sober smile creeping onto his face.

"You're going to need to be as tough as you've ever been."

"And you?"

He thought for a moment.

"I'll take it when it comes."

That was it. My friend had just come across the country to, among other things, say goodbye. He stood first, then I did. We came around the outdoor table and hugged each other in the cold. After a quick moment Neil stepped back. A sheen glistened his eyes slightly.

"I had to tell you," Neil said. "I'm violating maybe a dozen laws doing this, but how's that going to matter when it all hits the fan?"

"You don't trust the phones either, do you?"

He shook his head.

"They're listening. For key phrases. They'd be all over me, *and* you, an hour after we hung up."

"I can't believe this," I said.

"A lot of people won't. Then they'll die."

"Will it matter?" I asked. "If it's like you say, with no recovery, then eventually..."

Eventually even those who'd prepared would turn to dust. There was only a finite amount of stored food on the planet. If the stuff that was processed and jammed into cans ran out, so would the cans.

But Neil held the trump card in this musing on futility. It was not a question of being tough where an absolute obstacle intervened, but it was a question of something beyond the plans, the preparations, the determination to survive.

"There's always hope," he said. "Someone might figure this out. After everything's gone, in some bunker somewhere, maybe some genius kid with a chemistry set will put the pieces together."

Maybe...

That was a hell of a thin hope for saving the human race.

"Where do you go from here, Neil?"

"Back to D.C." he answered. "Back to the job. For a day. Then I'm outta there. I'm going to bring my dad to my place and..."

I nodded. Then I half chuckled, the rest a shocky gasp. Ten minutes ago a dear friend had shown up unannounced. Now I was saying goodbye, forever. And not just to him. To life as it was known.

"Don't delay," Neil said. "Don't think you have time just because it's relatively quiet. By the time they give the signal, it will be too late."

He could tell by the look on my face he'd tossed me a curveball. With a helluva a lot of topspin.

"When the tipping point is inevitable, there'll be a signal," he explained. "So essential personnel will know to head for collection points. From there they'll be transported to secure locations to carry on. Senators, representatives, other bureaucrats. Military leadership. They'll all gather and keep what's left of the country running. Until there's nothing left to run."

"What sort of signal?"

He shook his head.

"I don't know. They don't even know. This is longstanding protocol for emergencies that require the evacuation of the government. The principals are told to stay aware, and when the signal is given, there'll be no mistaking it."

"And everyone else?"

"It won't matter," he said, then took a slow breath and fixed a hard gaze upon me. "You've gotta hang on, Fletch. Okay? You have to. Stay alive."

"Jesus, Neil..."

He stepped back.

"Take care of yourself."

Then he was gone. Speeding out of the lot in his rental and down the street. I stood there in the chill for a moment, alone, wanting what had just transpired to be just some dream. Some waking hallucination. But when I looked back to the table we'd sat at, my friend's cup of coffee was still there.

This was really happening.

Three

Back at work I watched trucks roll in and out of the yard. I watched employees scurry about, performing their duties. Taking moments to socialize as everyone did occasionally during the day. These were people who depended upon me, and I upon them. Almost every single one of them was a friend. Not close like Neil, but we'd shared joy and sorrow together. Birthdays and funerals. I saw them five days out of seven, sometimes more.

And, most likely, they were all going to die if what Neil had told me was right.

Stop.

I had to tell myself this. I had to force the folly of doubt from my thoughts. Neil would not have traveled across the country to tell me what he had unless he was certain. So I either had to accept it as an event sure to come and act accordingly, or simply wait for the inevitability to roll over me, and all those near me, like a rising tide, drowning us slowly, inch by inch.

I wanted to live. There had to be hope, if not at the moment then somewhere down the road. But for that to matter I had to be around. I had to survive. So that is what I chose to do.

Out the window of my office my gaze found two things—our small box truck and the five-hundred gallon towable diesel tank. The former we used to pick up and deliver smaller items to job sites, such as finished lumber and anything electronic or fragile that needed to be kept out of the elements. The latter would often be towed, fully filled, to job sites distant from convenient service stations so that equipment could be refueled easily and quickly. Now I saw both of these things as vital to my survival.

* * *

In a sense I was flying blind. I had experience in survival, the same anyone who hunted the woods of Montana did, or should. Somewhat more than those whose idea of hardship was surviving an outage caused by icy limbs snapping from trees and felling power lines. But how did one prepare for the extent of carrying on that Neil described would be necessary? How?

One step at a time, I told myself.

As I'd shared with Neil, the MREs and other meager emergency supplies at my property were the extent of my preparation for unforeseen circumstances. I needed more. A lot more.

I'd driven by the store on the edge of town occasionally, never giving it more than a passing glance. *Bunker Bo's*, it was called, and from the signage plastered inside its front windows it was clear that its clientele tended toward the tinfoil hat crowd. Guys who feared the end of days. Global pandemics. Solar storms.

Or citizens getting gunned down at checkpoints, or shot from the sky.

Who was wearing the tinfoil hat now?

A clerk named Eddie greeted me warmly and immediately offered assistance. I declined his help for the moment, sharing that I wanted to wander about for a while. This I did, focusing my attention on what I believed to be the most important items for my long-term survival—food and water. I studied the cost and makeup of entire pallets of stable food caches, cases and cases of canned foodstuffs combined to offer all that an individual or family would need to stay alive for six months, a year, two years. The desired survival time was limited only by how much one was willing to spend. I had already decided to use all the resources I had available. Doing so wasn't difficult once you accepted that money would have little tangible meaning in a very short time.

When I was ready I approached Eddie and informed him there were three pallets of long-term food I would be getting. His eyes bugged a bit at the sizable order, and he asked me if I was certain I wanted that much. I deflected the inquiry with a lie. My company, I told him, was going to donate a large amount of stable food for relief efforts in Guatemala. A terrible landslide had recently poured down a valley there and the need to assist the survivors was obvious. In fact, I had already made a monetary donation for just this purpose. Now it seemed that might only offer short-term solace, since long-term was a concept about to lose most meaning for just about everyone. Day to day would be the mode of survival for those unprepared.

I was not going to be one of those.

With the food order out of the way I asked Eddie about water storage and filtration. There was a pond and feeder streams on my property, and a well that provided adequate supply. But I wanted to be ready in case something affected those, or the quality of what they offered. Eddie showed me powered filtration systems to remove most contaminants, and higher end models tailored to treat water with bacteria as well as other harmful impurities. He also described a gravity system, through which uncertain water would flow from an upper tank to a lower basin, passing through a series of natural and synthetic filters as it descended. Then he showed me smaller individual filters that one could use to sip directly from a body of water, no different than drinking through a straw. All these had advantages and disadvantages, he explained, and when he was done I told him I would take two of each. Again his eyes bugged a bit, and he commented that my compassion for the refugees was admirable.

Before I left I added a pallet of MREs to the order. Meals Ready to Eat, often called Meals Rarely Edible by soldiers in the field, for whom they'd been designed to sustain, were, to me, not bad at all. Many a hunting and camping trip I'd taken them along and been completely satisfied. Here and now, having them on hand could do no harm in addition to the larger cache I was building.

The box truck I'd brought from work was loaded by Eddie and another worker, forklift positioning the pallets and boxes, ties securing the load. I paid for the items, totaling just over $27,000, with a card that drew on my business credit line. If I was going all-in, there was no sense pretending there'd be a bill to pay come next month.

From *Bunker Bo's* I swung by an electrical supply house and purchased eight solar panels, spare inverter, wiring, and the hardware to mount the additional equipment alongside the eight panels I already had at my getaway. Two dozen deep cycle batteries completed my order and put another sizable dent in my credit line. I wasn't done gathering what I needed, but what I'd filled the truck with was the bulk of what I believed I'd need.

Fully loaded, I drove north from Missoula, skirting Flathead Lake, passing through Kalispell and turning west off the highway several miles past Whitefish. Nearly five hours it had taken me just to reach the driveway of my property. Next I had to break down what I'd bought so it could be unloaded by hand, my only option. An hour into the endeavor I began to wish for a forklift. By the second hour, though, the strain, both mental and physical, began to morph into some sort of drive I'd never known. Some energy that allowed me to carry and cart most of the food into my house, and the mechanical items into the barn. After six hours, with midnight approaching, I finally finished, sore but satisfied, the steps I'd taken toward my own survival adding meaning to the endeavor. I was reliant on myself. I wondered how many others would be able to say the same in the coming weeks and months.

I also wondered how many would be left.

Giving in to exhaustion I spent the night at my getaway, and rose early the next morning to return to Missoula. Over the next two days I made more trips, transporting what I believed would become essentials, including my ATV on a small flatbed trailer, and a half-dozen full five gallon gas cans with fuel stabilizers added. And, on my final trip, the tank trailer loaded with five hundred gallons of diesel fuel. Its absence was noted by my chief foreman, as was my own.

* * *

"You're not leveling with me," Marco said.

He stood just inside my office, the hum of activity from workers in the break room down the hall filtering in. They were laughing over some idiotic joke that I would normally chuckle at. But with my foreman of eight years staring at me, clearly worried, the humor landed flat.

"I'm not following you, Marco," I told him, feigning composure as best I could.

He stepped further into my office and closed the door behind.

"It's Thursday," Marco said. "Monday you get a visit from some old friend and the next thing I know the truck I need for the Peyton job is gone, and you're the one who took it. Two days later the truck's back, but the fueling trailer is gone. And it's still gone. But now you're here, and I'm left trying to figure out what the hell's going on."

Marco was no idiot. He was also a friend. A friend who deserved to know not only what I was doing, but why, and to what end. But if I opened my mouth to him, there was no telling where it would go from there. The information. The warning.

A warning whose origin could be traced back to Neil. Would a government willing to shoot down citizens at checkpoints hesitate to bring some wrath upon an employee who'd leaked a vital secret? Yes, I knew. They would. I couldn't risk his life for the sake of satisfying my foreman's worry.

Then again, he might not buy it at all. He could just as easily conclude that I'd gone slightly crazy. But with what we'd witnessed, both in person and in news reports, I had to think he might very well accept what I was relaying as gospel.

But what if it wasn't? There was still that slight chance that nothing of the magnitude I feared was going to happen. A chance that it would not all come tumbling down. I knew I couldn't bank on that, however. And I couldn't count on Marco keeping close what every instinct would tell him to share, just as it was telling me to.

"Just some things I have to deal with, Marco. One thing where my personal life and professional life have come together."

He eyed me skeptically.

"And the fuel trailer is essential to fixing whatever this issue is?"

"I know it doesn't make a lot of sense to you," I told him, the statement only partially a lie. "But it makes sense to me. And it is my fuel trailer."

That statement of rank, something I'd rarely, if ever, used before, seemed to trouble him more than the uncertainty my actions had caused.

"Okay," Marco said, and left my office, leaving the door open as he headed down the hallway, more laughter drifting in. Raucous laughter. It was sound of people without a care in the world.

* * *

I stayed late at the end of the day. When the last dispatcher left just after seven I was still at my desk, sitting, thinking, and wondering if this was the last time I would see the business I'd built. The business I'd struggled and sacrificed to nurture from a one-man contracting enterprise to a multimillion dollar powerhouse that allowed eighty workers to put food on the table for their families. Would the need for my business even exist in a month, a week, or the next morning? I didn't know, but I also didn't want to leave without taking in the feel of the place one last time.

In case this was the last time.

Four

I was ready to bug out.

I'd gathered and stored everything I could at my getaway. Whether that was everything I would need only time would tell. In the bed of my pickup, secured under the shell, I had the final boxes of clothing, medicine, and other items ready to go with me on my run to what I hoped would be a safe place. If safety was not what it offered in full, I was prepared for that eventuality with a selection of weapons and ammunition alongside the more mundane necessities. Pistols, rifles, and shotguns to complement what was already stashed on my property.

The only thing left to decide was when. When I would leave this world and this life behind. I'd continued to go to work each day. To play at living. Business continued. My workers demolished old buildings and put new ones up.

But enough ominous signs had appeared on the news since Neil's warning to me just over a week ago to convince me that what he feared was coming to pass. A complete quarantine of the nation was in effect. The borders, both North and South by land, and East and West by sea, were closed, patrolled now not by shifts of Border Patrol agents, but by units of the military that had been hardened by battles in Iraq and Afghanistan. It was a daily occurrence now to hear of fighter jets chasing away stray aircraft approaching the border, either accidentally or by design. Two more had been shot down, if what was being reported told the entire story. It could have been ten, or twenty. The press, whose freedom had been enshrined in the Constitution, seemed, at every turn, to be actively embracing anything the government said, and repeating it to a populace seeking assurances.

Assurances that, more and more, were ringing hollow.

But the news, the truth, or some semblance of it, was getting out. Between the rumors filling every corner of the internet, incidents were getting play. A news crew from an Alabama station had been shot by contract security while attempting to record the transfer of food from a supermarket chain warehouse to Blackhawk helicopters. Three journalists lay dead in a parking lot beneath the wash of rotor blades, but nowhere did that appear on national, or even local news. The video, captured by a frightened jogger in the right place at the wrong time, became the hottest topic on nearly every social media platform.

Until it disappeared.

For days afterword, those who had downloaded it attempted to post it again, only to have it disappear in a feat of digital magic whose origin was apparent to anyone with half a brain. But by then, more reports, often with video or photos to augment their authenticity, were flooding the internet. Not every bit of damning evidence of a government running amok could be done away with. The depth of the crisis was beginning to creep into the collective consciousness of the nation. People were scared. Checkpoints had become rife with standoffs. The disconnect between the governed and those who governed had become very, very real.

And very dangerous.

Something within told me I should go. Not in an hour, or a day, or two days, but that very minute. In the dark as the day spun down toward midnight, I should get in my truck and go. So strong was the feeling that I had walked around my home all evening with the keys to my pickup in my pocket.

I did not, however, want to give in to fear, regardless of what I knew had to be coming. Logic should inform the moment of my departure. As long as the situation was relatively stable, everyday living would be easier right where I was.

Stable, though, seemed more and more relative to the reality engulfing society. The news droned on that evening with story after story of the spiraling situation. Looting had begun in Oakland. Rioters were fired upon by police in San Antonio. A train in Indiana had been derailed, the contents of its boxcars carted off by hundreds of nearby residents. People who, until recently, would have reported such an act to authorities, were now participants, maybe out of some need for food that might have been aboard, or simply because they, too, felt that some tipping point was nearing and it was time to grab whatever was there for the taking.

I turned off the news and went to bed just after midnight, drifting off soon after, a combination of physical and mental weariness dragging me down to sleep. Dreams of football and high school and Neil soothed me. Drowsy memories of good times.

The respite from the real lasted just two hours.

Part Two

The Red Signal

Five

At ten after two in the morning my cell phone buzzed on the night stand, the grating sound dragging me up from sleep. My eyes opened to a room I'd expected to be dark. It wasn't. A reddish glow was spread upon the ceiling to the left of my bed, directly above my phone.

I rolled and took the vibrating device in hand. A bright red rectangle glared at me from the screen, nearly filling it. It buzzed again in my hand, as if a text or call was coming in. But none was. The thing had glitched, I told myself. Like the tiny computer it was. Likely it needed the same medicine that often cured its larger brethren when they electronically misbehaved, so I switched the power button off to reboot it.

But it stayed on. The grating vibration stopped, but the screen remained on. I tried again to shut it down, and again it didn't respond. It was either suffering from a major fault or...

... when the signal is given, there'll be no mistaking it.

Neil's words. Was he that knowledgeable? Or that prophetic?

Once again I tried to shut the phone down, and it refused.

Beyond the windows of my bedroom, in the distance, a chorus of sirens began to sound, rising and joining, wailing in unison as they moved across the city. Police and fire units, it seemed. Racing in convoy to the north. Toward the airport.

I kept my phone in hand and climbed out of bed, heading to the great room of my house, TV dominating what was, essentially, my man cave. I snatched the remote from the coffee table and turned it on. The sixty inch screen hummed and washed up from darkness until a bright red rectangle nearly filled it.

"Shit," I said, the word coming as mostly breath.

...there'll be no mistaking it.

I tried other stations, every station, from 24 hour news to reality TV, and all that I saw was that stretched square of red. The remote slipped from my hand and thudded softly on the floor.

"Shit," I muttered this time, almost under my breath, the word seeming the only true reaction I could muster at the moment.

Quickly I went to the kitchen and turned on the small radio I kept there, the channel permanently fixed to the sports talk station that was my company while I cooked late night suppers for myself. Sound rose from its small speaker. A sound that was not the chatter of voices. Wasn't the replay of some earlier show to fill the overnight hours. All there was was a single word, repeating over and over in a woman's monotone voice.

"Red... Red... Red..."

A second of silence filled the pause between each utterance of the word. The color.

The signal.

Here, too, I tried more channels. Each and every one spat the same three words at me.

"Red... Red... Red..."

I turned away from the radio and stared into the great room at television's screen, still blazing red. For a while I didn't move. More sirens screamed. A helicopter raced low overhead. Then another. And another.

"Red... Red... Red..."

The radio droned on.

You've gotta move.

I told myself that. The time had actually come. This life, whatever it was now, would not be that when the sun came up.

"Red... Red... Re—"

I switched the radio off, then returned to the great room and powered the television down.

Go.

The directive came again from within. Yet I felt no urgency nearer the surface where my thoughts were swimming. Just as I hadn't wanted to abandon the business I'd built as soon as I'd readied myself to bug out, here, in my home, I didn't want to disappear into the night. Maybe it was fear working on me. The desire to remain anchored to the familiar.

Or maybe there was that last bit of lingering hope that, if not a bad dream, all that was transpiring would, in short order, work itself out. The powers that be would actually function as they should and protect the populace. Life would go on.

A second train of sirens racing out of the city convinced me otherwise.

I dressed and slipped my pistol into the holster inside my waistband. The Springfield 1911 was condition one— cocked and locked. A flick of my thumb when drawing it would take the safety off and bring it to condition zero, ready to fire, something I sincerely hoped would not be necessary. I slipped into my coat and filled an ice chest with all the fresh and frozen food I could fit from the fridge, then grabbed the keys to my pickup and walked quickly to the door that led from the house to the garage. While it might have seemed logical to linger here for a moment, even more so than the time I'd taken at the business I'd built, I did not. The door to the house closed behind me and a minute later I was on my way. Leaving my old life behind.

* * *

The radio in my pickup droned the same signal.

"Red... Red... Red..."

I scanned the stations, every single one up and down both AM and FM bands, but nothing was being broadcast but those three words. It was clear to me that not every broadcaster had conspired to spread the signal. Some larger entity had stepped in and seized the ability to do so, as they had with the cell phones, and the television stations. A behemoth. NSA, CIA, DoD, it could have been any of them. Or none. Perhaps some blacker than black government agency was making this possible. Had been conceived years earlier to be ready for just such an eventuality. Just such a need.

And people had thrown fits about some functionary reading their text messages. They should have looked deeper. Representatives should have demanded accountability. Journalists should have exposed the whole truth. People should have done their jobs.

Now the fruits of invasive secrecy were plain as day. To me, at least. They were being used so that the few might survive, at the expense of the many. Rather than being straight with the country as a whole, lies and misdirections had allowed the elite to see to their own preparations. For their own purposes. The ordinary American had no time to prepare—physically, emotionally, spiritually.

The moment had come and we were being failed by the very institutions founded to serve us.

"Red... Red... Red..."

I turned the radio down, but not off, wanting to know at the very first instant if something other than the signal was allowed to broadcast. Neil had said to pay attention. To be aware. Now that the first indications of the crises exploding had arrived, that advice seemed even more relevant. Information would have to get out, from some sources, for as long as possible. It was human nature to connect, to share. Even though I was going into this alone, I was still part of the whole. My place in the human race hadn't left me, even if I was separating myself from it for a while.

Heading north, I left Missoula behind, a single Trooper racing south toward the city in his Highway Patrol cruiser passing me as the dimmed lights of the city at night faded in my rearview. I passed through Arlee, and by the spot of the checkpoint massacre, three small crosses hammered into the earth on the road's shoulder, one snapped backward with purpose. Someone had made a statement at the makeshift memorial site. It wasn't hard to imagine which lost soul that desecrated marker represented.

Traffic picked up as I cruised through Kalispell near five in the morning. More lights were on in residential neighborhoods than should have been at the hour. A police car was stopped mid-intersection, lone officer outside, halting cars as they came through, spending a few seconds conversing with each driver before letting them continue. I pulled up and rolled down my window as I came to a stop.

"Sir, good morning."

"Officer," I said, the low repetition of '*Red... Red... Red...*' just audible from my radio.

"You already know that something's up."

I nodded. He glanced up and down the street. No cars but mine at the moment.

"Most people I've talked to don't know," he shared, then reached to the radio on his belt and dialed up the volume.

"Red... Red... Red..." the signal sounded, just as it was on the plain radio receiver in my pickup. Then transmissions from police dispatch filled a carved-out silence between the words, until they repeated again, some accommodation of official communications obviously made.

"Nothing good's happening, officer," I told him, and now he nodded. Some clear resignation about him.

"You headed north?"

"Yeah. Past Whitefish."

He considered that for a moment. Another car neared, slowing to stop behind me. The officer gave its driver a quick wave and then focused on me again.

"That might be a dicey route," he said. "That's why I'm stopping people. A broadcast went to out Highway Patrol to shut down access north out of Whitefish."

"The border's already closed," I said.

"Maybe not anymore. An hour ago a couple Blackhawks flew down from that way and unloaded a bunch of soldiers just outside of town. They hurried onto trucks and headed west."

"They pulled the unit sealing the border?"

"That's my guess. Probably why they're stopping people at Whitefish with Highway Patrol. It's a natural chokepoint."

They...

Orders were being given from on high. A plan was being set in motion. Troops were being pulled for other duties.

"Red... Red... Red..."

He turned his radio back down.

"I just wanted to give a heads up that you may hit some trouble up that way."

"I appreciate the warning," I said, and he stepped back. I pulled away, glancing to my rearview to see the officer leaning down, talking to the driver of the car that had pulled in behind me. At that moment I couldn't help but marvel at the sight of a public servant behaving as though he knew who he really worked for.

* * *

Forty minutes later I arrived in Whitefish and cruised through the waking town, sunrise hinted at by the bluish glow to the east. But there was another glow ahead, yellow lights blinking. Warning beacons atop barriers that were erected across the road, police cars behind them, officers milling about in the chill of the coming dawn, turning cars away. The way out of town was blocked.

I turned off to a side street and pulled in behind a row of shops that had once been rustic staples, but were now trendy outlets of whatever tourists were craving. I killed the engine and thought for a moment. Thought on the situation. Just as the officer in Kalispell had warned, the way north out of Whitefish was shut down. Yet, that was where I had to go.

A few blocks to the north were railroad tracks, and beyond that a road that followed the gentle curve of Whitefish Lake—for a short distance. Just shy of Dog Bay that road ended.

But the railroad tracks continued.

That was the way. I just had to hope the powers that be had thrown up just the one roadblock. But in case they hadn't, I hopped from my truck and went to the rear, crouching at the bumper and gripping the license plate, pulling and twisting at the thin slab of metal. It would not break, but the screws that mounted it did give, slipping from their anchors. In a minute I had the only thing that outwardly identified my truck as belonging to me in hand. I tossed it in the back seat as I got in and fired up the engine, sitting for a moment, steeling myself for the run ahead as the truck idled. If an officer of the law did spot me evading the roadblock, there would be no license plate to lead them to me, and eventually to my property up the highway. Still, if they spotted me, would they chase me? And, if they chased me, would I run?

"Yes," I said aloud, and shifted into drive, pulling back onto the side street, then back onto Lion Mountain Road, Route 93, the main route in and out of Whitefish. The way I had to go. Past the roadblock ahead.

I drove slowly toward it. The last of the cars preceding me turned around and headed back into town. Two State Troopers stood at the barricade, waiting for me. One held a patrol rifle, an AR-15 like the one on floor just to my right, low and ready. Ready for any trouble. For any situation.

Like the one I was about to present him with.

I gripped the steering wheel tight, prepared to swing it hard right. My foot eased from the brake to the accelerator, ready to mash it to the floor.

But I did neither. The roar from my left stopped me. I pressed the brake again and looked out the side window just as an old International Harvester Scout, its top cut away, rumbled past in the lane meant for oncoming traffic. Its four seats were filled, with two more passengers crammed into the small cargo space behind. All men. All carrying long guns.

"Oh man..."

The Scout stopped twenty yards short of the checkpoint, Troopers lining the barricade now at the sight of the mini armada, six men climbing from the vehicle. Four took positions behind it. One slipped right, threading the space between me and the car behind. The final man walked to the front of the Scout and stood there, cradling an AK-47, eyeing the Troopers as they began to scream orders at him and the others. More Troopers maneuvered for cover. The men behind the Scout spread out, covering the movement.

This would not be another Arlee, I realized. It would be worse. Much worse. And I was positioned perfectly to catch a fair amount of fire once it began. From the looks of the men who'd come to challenge the roadblock, fire would most certainly begin.

Soon.

In an instant I made the decision, flooring it and swinging hard right, off the road, tearing through a low chain link fence and onto the browning greens of the golf course. I sped across the rolling landscape, following the cart path, threading between trees at the northern border of the course. Another chain link fence shredded as I punched through it and skidded across State Park Road, blue and red lights sweeping the intersection with Lakeshore Road to the east—another roadblock.

I had been right. The railroad tracks were the only way. And they were dead ahead. I steered straight and accelerated toward them.

Six

My pickup bounced over the railroad tracks and slid on the gravel embankment beyond. Behind, for the first time since the signal, I heard gunshots. They cracked in the distance. Faint screams followed. Then the roar of engines, followed by more shots. Dozens. Then hundreds. Then the crunch of metal, speeding car meeting still object.

I steered north and followed along the embankment, tracks to my left on the rise, Dog Bay to my right, a tickle of morning reflected blue upon its rippling surface. The *whoop whoop* of sirens filled the waning darkness, backup racing to the checkpoint, the worst having played out. Citizen or citizens down, maybe dead. Maybe officers of the law as well.

Anarchy, I thought, though I feared it was worse than that.

They were blocking the main road. Blocking the back roads. And they were willing to kill to enforce that blockade. To me that seemed a bit beyond mere anarchy. And I wanted to avoid it as best I could, so I followed the embankment, keeping the raised rail bed between me and the parallel roads beyond. It shielded me from view, and before long the mayhem in Whitefish was behind me. I had made it.

Then I saw the lights.

Spokes of red and blue swept through the towering trees, coming from the far side of the tracks. I slowed and nosed my pickup into a clearing almost at the water's edge, killing the engine. Through the open window I heard radio chatter, coming from the same point of origin as the lights. At distance it was difficult to grasp every morsel of the rapid communications, police units talking to dispatch, and vice versa, with interruptions from fire, National Guard, and a half-dozen other entities cramming the mutual aid frequency.

And, every so often, the frequency would be taken over, and three words would be broadcast, plain as day.

"Red... Red... Red..."

The chatter would then start again, until the next interruption. Still, though, I couldn't understand the transmissions as far away as I was, so I eased from my pickup and quietly closed the driver's door, just enough to kill the dome light. I could have taken my AR with me, but those were police on the other side of the rise. If they noticed me, I didn't want to be seen as a threat. They were enough on edge as it was. The pistol concealed on my hip beneath my coat was all I was willing to chance.

I hoped there'd be no need to put it to use. Not here. Not against them.

Less than a minute of quiet walking along the tree line brought me to the side of the rise just opposite the police cars. The back and forth on the radio was clearer here. Talk about securing the airport. The arrival of the governor. Air Force plane waiting for him.

Essential personnel...

I imagined the governor of a state could be considered essential. A military aircraft tasked to whisk him off would seem to confirm that.

But he was in Helena, the state capital. I'd seen a news conference just that morning with his stoic face seeming worn, trying to assure the citizens of the state that all was being done in cooperation with the federal government to manage the situation. That was hundreds of miles away.

What the hell were police doing here, stopped on a back road?

"Red... Red... Red..."

I crept up the embankment toward the tracks, eyes peeking over the steel rails. Just beyond the opposite embankment I could see the two State Troopers, their cars angled across the road, blocking it, lights flashing to warn anyone approaching of the barricade.

"What's your wife doing?" the younger Trooper asked his colleague.

The older man shrugged and shook his head. All about him was tight, like a wound spring.

"Haven't been able to reach her."

"Yeah," the younger Trooper said, taking his cell phone in hand. It cast a familiar red glow up upon his face. "My Sherry's gotta be freaking out."

"She's probably still asleep," the older Trooper said. "By the time she wakes up this will all be sorted out."

"Yeah," the younger Trooper agreed, no belief at all in the word.

The hot white of headlights whipped around a turn and raced at the Troopers. The older man put a hand on his pistol and stepped in front of the cruiser barricade, holding a palm out to the approaching car. It stopped and a frantic man jumped out.

"Get back in your car, sir, and turn around!" the older Trooper commanded.

"I've got to get to Eureka!" the frantic man pleaded. "My mother's in Eureka, and she's sick!"

Eureka was just south of the Canadian border. A quick drive up the highway. But the older Trooper wasn't going to budge.

"The road is closed, sir, now turn around and head south."

The frantic man walked forward, past the front of his car, closing on the older Trooper.

"Back in your car!" the older Trooper shouted, drawing his pistol and taking aim at the frantic man.

I couldn't believe it. I was going to witness it yet again. Another citizen getting gunned down for no more than doing what they had every right to do. Could I just lay there on the cold gravel slope behind the rails and watch this? And do nothing?

"I have to get to her!"

The younger Trooper drew his weapon and joined his partner.

"Back to your car or we will shoot!" the older Trooper threatened. To his right his partner's gaze shifted fast between him and the man defying them. There was a fear about the younger Trooper. A sense of incredulity, almost. As if he'd woken that day and stepped into some bizarre, twisted version of the life he'd known.

"Please," the frantic driver begged.

The older Trooper's finger slid onto the trigger.

Christ, I thought, and reached beneath my coat to my holstered pistol. In another time not long before, the motion I made would have been inconceivable. Even the thoughts instantly filling my head were impossible to immediately accept as my own. I was thinking, with clarity and conviction, that there was no way I could let the police shoot the stranger. In no way could I simply be a silent witness. My fingers slid around the weapon and began easing it from its holster.

That is when it happened.

Beneath me, the compacted slope of gravel and stone shifted, my body moving with it, setting off a minor avalanche of rocks that clicked as they tumbled down the embankment.

"What was that?" the older Trooper asked, glancing toward the darkness that shrouded me.

"I don't know," the younger Trooper said, sidestepping my way.

Dammit...

I had to react, rolling fast down the embankment and scrambling to my feet.

"Hey!"

The shout came from behind, the younger Trooper calling out to me as I disappeared into the trees. I dodged between the pines like opponents on the gridiron, pistol in hand, hoping desperately that I would not have to use it. I'd been ready to act to stop more violence upon an innocent, but direct conflict on my own, for my own skin, was what I wanted to avoid. Running to safety was how I had started this after the Red Signal, and that was how it needed to end, getting the hell out of harm's way and to my refuge.

I reached my truck and started it up, holstering my weapon as a flashlight swept the landscape deep in the trees. The Trooper, the younger one, I imagined, had been dispatched by his partner to chase me down and bring me in.

That wasn't going to happen.

Keeping my lights off I backed away from the trees and sped away, racing past the spot on the embankment where I'd given my position away. A glance in my rearview revealed the younger Trooper emerging from the trees at a dead run, then stopping when he saw me pulling away.

I raced along the tracks, woods shielding the lake to my right, driving as fast as the sometimes narrow trail I was blazing allowed. Miles further on I neared Lazy Bay and the road that dead-ended there. Several miles on, past remote houses and walls of forest thick enough to blot out the coming day, I finally reached Route 93 and headed north.

Barely a mile down the highway I saw the red and blue lights racing at me from behind. Just one cruiser. Catching up fast.

There was no point in trying to outrun my pursuer. My pickup was built for load, not speed. I was out of good options.

Except one.

I slammed on the brakes and slid my pickup to a stop, its length skidding to block both lanes of the highway, dull metal guard rails to either side, creating a makeshift roadblock. The cruiser in pursuit screamed to a stop, tires smoking as they grabbed asphalt. By the time it sat motionless a dozen yards from my pickup I was out, AR-15 in hand, taking dead aim at the younger Trooper as he stepped fast from his cruiser and drew down on me from behind the open driver's door.

"Put down your weapon!" he commanded me.

I made no move to comply.

"Now!" he shouted, using volume to exert authority.

"No," I said.

I'm not sure what he expected me to do or say, but the simple word of defiance appeared to take him aback. He shifted in place, gaze sweeping the road to either side. Possibly to see if he'd fallen for some planned ambush. Or maybe he just wanted a way out of what was happening.

"What's your name?" I asked past the triangle glowing in my AR's illuminated sight.

He hesitated for a moment, fingers flexing around his pistol.

"Trooper Morris."

"No," I told him. "Your name."

"Jason," he said, a slight catch in his words.

"Jason, listen to me. Something's happening, something big, and people are scared. You're scared. I'm sure as hell scared. But that doesn't mean either of us has to do the wrong thing."

"I'm just following—"

"Orders," I said for him. "I know. Your partner back there probably told you to go corral my ass and drag it back to the roadblock. Right?"

He nodded sharply. Like a frightened child might confirm an innocent misdeed they'd been caught in.

"Him telling you that, or even higher-ups ordering these roadblocks, those things don't make it right. None of it." I knew what I had to say next. "And killing you wouldn't be the right thing for me to do, either."

I could see the color drain slightly from his already pale complexion.

"The smart thing for me to do, to have done, to make sure you didn't know where I was going, would be to pump you full of bullets before you ever had the chance to get out of your cruiser. But I didn't. I couldn't. That would not be defending myself. That would be executing you. I've seen that done, and I don't want to go there. I don't even want to come close to that mental place where one person can do that to another. So let's end this."

"What do you mean?" he asked, truly at a loss.

"We walk away," I told him. "You go back and report that you couldn't locate me, and I go on my way, as I should have been able to do in the first place. The world is going to shit, Jason. You and I killing each other isn't going to change that. It's only going to put that stench on us for doing so."

Behind him, the radio in his cruiser spat out "Red... Red... Red..."

"We're both better than this, Jason," I told him, and for a long moment in the half-light he stared at me, until finally the aim of his weapon dropped, muzzle pointed at the asphalt between us.

"What the hell is happening?" he asked, truly asked, almost a plea. Just some young kid, probably a year out of the academy. "Is this all because of the blight?"

"Yeah," I said, and watched him holster his pistol, my AR coming down as the moment fully defused.

"What the hell do I do?"

"You could do your job," I told him. "Or you could get with your family and try to make it through this."

He thought on the suggestion for a moment, then nodded. It was a quiet gesture. A confirmation closer to surrender than determination. Whatever decision he'd made bringing no full measure of comfort.

"Go on, Jason," I calmly urged him.

He slipped back into his cruiser and killed the pulsing red and blue lights atop the vehicle, staring at me through the windshield for a moment before backing through a three point turn and speeding south down the highway. When he was out of sight beyond a low rise in the road, I returned to my pickup and continued north. I saw no lights in my rearview the rest of the way. No sign of life at all.

I wondered if Trooper Jason Morris would be the last person I'd ever see.

Seven

I turned off the road and drove maybe twenty yards up the driveway of my refuge and stopped, killing the engine and getting out, AR in hand as I waited. And listened. And watched.

No one had followed. No officers of the law had hung back, blacked out, trailing me covertly. Waiting for me to stop so they could pounce. I had made it. Jason had taken what I'd said to heart. He hadn't radioed for reinforcements.

I was home.

From the back of my pickup I dragged a stout chain and looped it around a sturdy pine on one side of the driveway, then around a similar tree opposite it, securing both ends with heavy padlocks. The linked barrier was set about radiator high, and would, if not stop any unexpected arrivals, at least let them know that their presence was not entirely welcome. Finished, I climbed back into my pickup and drove the hundred yards or so to my house. Again I stood quiet once outside my vehicle, taking in my surroundings. My new surroundings.

My forever surroundings, a small voice within suggested. Maybe warned.

It mattered not, I knew. The fact that I was here, alive, somewhat prepared. I slung my AR and took mental stock of what I'd accomplished already before arriving. Beyond the food and consumables I'd trucked up for storage, other practicalities had occupied me on the few trips I'd made up in the previous weeks.

In the barn, whose roof I'd mostly patched and siding I'd mended where needed, I'd installed a timed filter on the mobile tank filled with diesel, scheduled to run every day to mitigate the inevitable fouling of the fuel by moisture. How long that would keep the diesel viable I didn't know. Six months? A year?

That pump, and my house, depended for power on the solar array I'd expanded. Mounted out back of my house, with a full southern exposure, what it produced from sunlight was fed into a bank of batteries that had taken over the back bedroom. That was now power central, with distribution panel, inverters, and a switch allowing me to change the whole thing over to generator power if need be. That beefy unit, which I'd positioned in an old, well ventilated shed on the west side of the house, was probably the weakest link in my attempt to maintain some creature comforts. It was fifteen years old, and had, through my own fault, been neglected in the many years it had sat here, virtually unused. It was working now after some maintenance. I hoped it still would if it came to needing it.

For heating, there was an abundant supply of wood just outside my door. I'd already laid in two full cords for the coming winter, and with either chainsaw or axe I could take down whatever more I needed, hauling sized logs on the back of the ATV I'd trailered up the past weekend. Critical areas, where the batteries and electronics were situated, and in the barn near the diesel filter system, had dedicated 12 volt space heaters. Not enough to make the space anything near habitable for any stretch of time, but plenty to ward off any threat of freezing during the coldest periods.

All the preparations I'd made, both mechanical and practical, would require near constant maintenance. Snow would need to be cleared from the solar panels as it accumulated. Filters would need to be cleaned. Battery connections would have to be checked for corrosion. Food would have to be planned, and rotated, and kept free of assault by vermin.

And still, I knew I wasn't fully ready. I doubted anyone could be. Some things I was certain to forget, or be unaware of altogether. There would be failures. Breakdowns. Mistakes. If none of them killed me, I would consider myself lucky.

But I was here. Safe for the moment. With much to do. I made my way inside and lit a fire in the hearth of the great room, facing it from the old leather chair with a pad and pencil on my lap, ready to make my list for the first day of my new life. Tasks, large and small, to begin or complete. The myriad of necessary actions tumbled about in my head as I tipped it and let it loll toward the window, the day sweeping yellow over the trees and mountains beyond. Before I could stop myself my eyes began to flutter, then close, and I was dreaming. Visions filling the sleep as I fell into it, exhausted. Images and sounds of gunfire and blood and screams.

The new world.

Eight

More than two years earlier, on a lark, Neil and I had decided to spend a cold Sunday in February watching the Super Bowl at my getaway. All it had taken then was dragging a satellite dish to the property, mounting it, connecting it to an older flat screen I was ready to do away with, and, with Neil performing a little electronic larceny, jacking the converter box so we could 'borrow' the signal for a bit. The dish had remained mounted to the roof since, neglected, weather and nesting birds wreaking havoc upon it, but after waking from the exhaustion-fueled sleep that had seized me, a few hours of attention on the receiver as the afternoon crept toward evening gave me a window to the world outside.

None of the major stations were coming in on the satellite. No CNN, no ABC, nothing. I guessed it was possible that they were already off the air, without staff, some trouble spreading quickly. More likely, though, was a simple reality unrelated to what had happened—our little satellite signal theft had been shut down. The signal once again scrambled.

One station did come in, though. From Denver. A local network affiliate that displayed nothing more than a solid red rectangle on screen. No different than what I'd seen on my television at home.

At my old home.

I left the television on, ignoring what drain it might have on my batteries, and went to the hearth, arranging logs and setting the kindling beneath ablaze. In ten minutes I had a fire licking at the hearth's blackened interior. The old leather chair that faced it swallowed my still-tired body. To the left a side table filled the space between my chair and another, its emptiness stark and chilling.

Neil had sat there. With me. In front of a fire no different than the one that blazed before me now. We'd relaxed, tossed back beers, bullshitted after a day's fishing. Now I sat alone.

An overwhelming need to reach out to my friend filled me, and I dug my cell phone from my pocket, the act futile before ever seeing the NO SIGNAL displayed on the top of its screen. I knew there'd be no service at my refuge. There never had been. A few miles north of Whitefish things got spotty. Back in the woods, behind hills that rolled toward the mountains, one might as well have been trying to reach out from a black hole. But the desire to connect with him was impossible to resist, and I stared at the phone for several minutes before realizing that the visual representation of the Red Signal still filled most of the screen. Even without reception. Somehow the warning had been downloaded, and, for lack of a better term, lived within the device now.

I turned my cell phone over and laid it face down on the side table, regarding it warily for a moment, then looking to the fire again as I said a quiet prayer for my friend.

* * *

I stood in the kitchen and stared at the stove and cursed myself.

"Idiot."

The stove was perfectly good, but, like all stoves, it required fuel, and the propane tank nestled out back beyond the generator shed hadn't been topped off since spring. And, adding insult to injury, that slow leak I'd suspected it to have in its regulator, the one I'd been meaning to get fixed, looked to have bled out what remained after a spring and summer of regular use.

I cranked the burner off, then on again, and flicked the long lighter I held over the jets. A few spouts of flame glowed blue for a second, then flickered out, whatever gas there'd been in the tank virtually gone. I'd stocked up on smaller propane cylinders for a camp stove, and a dozen large bags of charcoal for the barbecue, but I'd mentally prepared myself for at least a few months cooking on the existing stove, in the kitchen, like any normal person would. Just a slice of my old life that I could maintain.

Wait...

I didn't speak the word aloud, but even thinking it I felt a sense of relief rise. *Possible relief.* From the moment of my arrival early in the day until this very moment, I hadn't opened the shutoff valve on the tank. The very same valve I'd closed at the end of my last extended stay during the summer. All I was getting was residual gas in the line between the tank and the house.

"Idiot," I repeated, for different reasons now, and tossed the lighter onto the kitchen table as I pushed the back door open roughly. I'd neglected to grab my jacket, and the evening chill was already settling in, biting at me as I moved down the side of my house and rounded the back corner. The propane tank, supported on its side like some giant white pill, rested just ahead, in the deep shadow laid by the generator shed, the very last light of day blotted out by the structure. I went to it and reached for the valve handle.

But I stopped before laying a hand upon it. Even in the din of the coming night I noticed something.

The regulator fixed to the outlet valve had been changed. It was dull metal and far from new, but it was different. Not the rusted mass that had topped the tank the last time I saw it.

I grabbed the valve handle and twisted it open. Gas hissed through the regulator and into the buried line feeding my house. The tank wasn't empty. The repair had prevented that from happening.

But repaired by who?

Instantly I felt exposed, turning to take in the sight of the darkened woods surrounding my refuge. I wore no pistol on my belt. Had no rifle slung. One or the other I should have had with me. Because, clearly, I wasn't the only person who'd visited my refuge in the recent past.

I glanced to the working regulator again, then returned to the house, closing the back door and locking it as night came fully. Gas was flowing again. The meal I'd planned from the small amount of fresh food I'd brought with me on this final trip was just minutes away. But I never cooked it. Never turned the stove on. Sounds from the great room made that impossible.

Voices.

Nine

The pair of newscasters, a man and a woman, stared out at me from the television in the great room, taking turns speaking to the camera as the newsroom buzzed behind. Everyone both intentionally and unintentionally on camera seemed running on the juice that fueled the news profession when some crisis struck.

Calm, though, was my reaction to seeing what I did. Borne of lingering tiredness, or simply from surprise at finding some connection to the world beyond my refuge, it set me into a mode of near stasis. I didn't sit. Didn't move. I just stood a few steps inside the great room and watched the first reports of the nation beginning to crumble.

"Again, bear with us," the male newscaster said. A graphic beneath identified him as Jim Winters, and his colleague as Stephanie Brent. "We've just managed to break through the signal that has apparently overrun all television broadcasts."

"And radio," Stephanie added as Jim took a breath. "Cell phones, the internet. This takeover of communications has been total and widespread."

"Unprecedented," Jim agreed, falling quickly back into his role. "If you are joining us, this is Network Five, Denver, and we are on the air after more than fourteen hours of inability to bring the news to you." He glanced briefly over his shoulder, to ranks of monitors high on the wall in the newsroom beyond, each and every one still showing the glaring red rectangle. "All national and affiliate stations are still off the air, as you can see behind me."

"If you pick up your landline phone," Stephanie said, retrieving a handset from beneath the sleek desk at which they sat, "you'll hear this."

She held the phone close to the small black microphone clipped to the collar of her blouse, and over the air the familiar repetition was broadcast.

"Red... Red... Red..."

"There are no dial tones," she said, returning the phone to its hidden cradle beneath the desk. "Just that word repeating over and over."

"It is the same for calling on cell phones," Jim told the audience. "Which has made our attempts to get some explanation from authorities exceedingly difficult. We've sent staff to reach out to both city and state officials, but have received no telling information."

"Our engineers aren't even sure how they were able to override the jamming signal," Stephanie admitted. "But, thankfully, they were."

They bantered on for a few minutes about their own situation at the station. How seasoned reporters were trying to work sources, to dig, to pressure any who might have information. But there was nothing concrete to offer. Only speculation.

"In the absence of official statements," Jim began, drawing a breath, as if steeling himself for some difficult admission, "we must look to events that might enlighten our understanding of this ongoing event. What do we actually know?"

He began to list facts of the moment, and facts that could very well help explain the situation. There was widespread concern about the blight. Concern that had begun to manifest itself in hoarding, shortages, even theft of foodstuffs from warehouses. If the seriousness of the blight and its effects had been concealed from the public, might not the Red Signal be related? Some alert from the government to personnel? Jim Winters surmised that this was precisely so. I knew it was, thanks to Neil.

"And just who has the ability, the power, to do what we see on those screens behind me? We've learned through leaks and reporting by the few brave journalists with guts enough to stand against a government that preaches openness while enforcing secrecy that agencies of our own intelligence apparatus have—"

Something just off camera drew Jim's attention for an instant, interrupting his monologue.

"No, I will not 'be careful'," Jim said, Stephanie at his side, both glaring at some unseen individual off camera. "We've been 'careful' for too long. It's time to tell it like it is." Again he looked to the camera. To the audience, whatever it numbered, beyond the lens. "Our own intelligence agencies have woven themselves into our daily existence. Hacking emails, collecting phone calls, tracking our movements both online and off with help from compliant technological behemoths. Is it too far-fetched to assume that an entity capable of that is also capable of implanting some code in our phones? Or taking over the airwaves? The satellites? To borrow a clichéd phrase, this reporter thinks not. So we have that as a starting point—this is the doing of our own government. And that, my friends, sends shivers down my spine. Because if they are afraid..."

He didn't go on. Or couldn't. After a moment to regain his composure, he simply glanced to Stephanie, and she took over.

"We have verified eyewitness reports that highways in and out of the Denver metropolitan area have been sealed by law enforcement," she said, a stern directness about her now. She seemed to sit straighter. To speak clearer. Like an elder delivering uncertain news to an extended family, telling them all hope was not lost—yet. "There have been incidents of force being used against people trying to both leave and enter the city."

So it was happening in Denver as well. Northern Montana did not have the monopoly on the first taste of a government tightening its grip. But wasn't that, if all that was supposedly coming turned out to be true, an endeavor no more useful than a man strangling himself?

I turned away from the TV and returned to the kitchen, making my dinner, some sausage and peppers, as the broadcast continued. Snippets of the new normal drifted in. Man and woman on the street interviews, people more confused than frightened at this stage. Video from a distance of muzzle flashes and the quickened crack of small arms fire, followed by a concussive explosion. Police tactical teams had been deployed, and were being used.

Then there was the looting. I returned to the great room with dinner plate in hand to watch this, sitting in front of the television now, picking at my food, taking in the images of windows being smashed, televisions being carted off, armfuls of clothes, cell phones and cameras. It had come to this quicker than I'd expected. Two, three days of worry I'd thought, then the breakdown would begin in earnest. But here, unmolested, the foul nature of some was surfacing, in concert with its accompanying idiocy. Televisions? Cameras? These were prime examples of what Darwin had suggested. While they should be stripping shelves of foodstuffs, these people were grasping at worthless baubles of infotainment. The value of yesterday, of last night, still rang true in their thoughts, their desires. They lived for the moment. They would die for it, as well.

And some already had. More video of store owners firing indiscriminately into crowds of looters and onlookers was shown. Bloodbaths unfolded across Denver, at the hands of authorities and terrified citizens fighting to protect what they'd worked for.

But it was all dust. Or soon would be. Fires raged into the night. Long after my dinner was eaten and the plate quickly washed, the news focused on infernos spreading downtown. Fire crews, stretched thin by the sheer mass of conflagrations, and by dwindling numbers as firefighters chose to protect their own families, were unable to stem the roiling orange tide that leapt from commercial areas to residential neighborhoods.

Denver was a city consuming itself. Civilization on a pyre. A beacon atop the Rockies to mark the beginning of the end.

Long past midnight, into the second full day after the Red Signal, Jim and Stephanie were still on the air, the anchors and those behind the scenes doing what news, regardless of bias, had always done well—bring the scope of a disaster into one's living room. I sat with them as their city, their home, smoked and screamed. Gunshots echoed even through their microphones. Close to the studio. After the first few times, neither flinched at the sound. They were exhausted. And numb.

What law there was had been tasked with sealing cities, blocking entrance and exit. Controlling movement. Or just plain controlling. For as long as they could. Their normal duties, protection, enforcement, prevention, had been set aside.

"All tumbling down," I said aloud, then said no more. I just watched. And listened.

"We'll be leaving you in a few minutes," Jim said, nodding to his co-anchor. "Ed Mills and Terry Goodwin will take over for us. Obviously we're not going back to any kind of regular programming. I'm not sure..." He hesitated, as if reconsidering the gravity of what he'd chosen to say. After a moment, he steeled himself and finished the thought. "I'm not sure we ever will."

It might have been the truest words ever spoken by a journalist.

Ten

Seven days passed before the Denver station went dark.

I spent that week completing tasks both large and small to prepare myself, and my refuge, for what lay ahead. Patching suspect areas of the barn roof. Weighing myself and making a chart of calories needed to maintain my weight at various levels of activity. Cutting felled trees and stacking the wood for the winter just around the corner. Running my truck, the generator, my ATV, all to make sure they were in working order and keep the internals lubricated.

But always the television was on. Twenty-four hours a day. Whether I was outside or in. I'd even taken to sleeping on the couch in front of it, fire burning in the hearth off to the side of the great room. A succession of names and faces rotated in and out of the anchor chair, the numbers dwindling over the days that followed the Red Signal. Jim Winters, though, was there to the end.

It happened on Thanksgiving, of all days. The last of my fresh food had been eaten two days earlier, and for the day, the holiday, I'd concocted a spread for myself cannibalized from both MREs and a portion of dehydrated chicken. Surprisingly, it wasn't bad, which didn't make it good, but, in the end, it was to mark the fact that I was alive. And I had that to be thankful for.

Jim Winters, though, was looking haggard and hungry, his face thinned, eyelids slack as he looked into the camera. I'd read somewhere once that there was just an eight day supply of food in the huge warehouses that supplied the supermarket chains. Store shelves would have been bought out or looted in the first few days after the Red Signal, and what was intended to replenish them had likely never made it out of the cavernous storage facilities that contained everything from canned corn to frozen slabs of ribs. Jim Winters himself had reported on just such facilities being raided by a panicked public, stripped to the rafters, nearly half of the food within destroyed in fights and fires that erupted over it. There simply was no more. The man looking out at me from the television was living proof of that.

"We are on generator power here at Network Five," Jim said, the heft of his voice seeming withered. What authority he could muster was fading. A sign of stoicism in the first few days after the crisis exploded, he now was little different than the tattered populace he served, wasting slowly physically, nearly shattered emotionally. There was no hope in his manner. He was going through the motions. "I am assured that we have adequate supplies for at least six days. Hopefully there will be some relief by...by then."

I'd finished my dinner. Hunger was nowhere in my thoughts. I'd prepared, and I'd been lucky. But I was the exception, not the rule.

"If you have food, ration it," Jim told his audience. "Stay home. Stay inside. If you have firearms, be ready. The police are not responding to any requests for help. As a captain told us in Mary Crane's interview yesterday, they have been tasked with containing residents to the city so that relief efforts can be centralized efficiently."

For a moment, Jim quieted. No co-anchor sat next to him. Stephanie hadn't been seen with him for two days. Behind, the hive of activity that had accompanied the station's breaking through the Red Signal was no more. Twenty staffers had become ten, which had become five, and which now, at most, was two. Silence embraced Jim during his pause, which only served to add gravity to what he said next.

"There will be no relief. We have been fed, and are being fed, lies. From where the decision to do this originated, I do not know. But it has come from higher authorities. This we can be certain of." He cleared his throat, openly and without any vanity, choking back emotion. "We are on our own."

Again he was quiet, then he glanced slightly off camera and gave a single nod.

"We're now going to play something recorded just this morning," Jim said, the statement coming as if he was releasing a breath he'd held for some time. "We debated showing you this, but you have a right to know the extent of what has begun happening. It came to us from a family returning to Denver after attempting to join relatives in Missouri."

Jim sat motionless for a moment as the segment queued up. Then he was gone, replaced by video of a long line of vehicles creeping eastward on Interstate 70, fleeing Denver in slow motion, brake lights blazing, something ahead impeding the flow of traffic.

Then it appeared. The reason for the slowdown. A helicopter, sweeping low in the distance ahead, seen through the windshield of the car from which the images were being recorded.

"Daddy, what is that?" a little girl asked, unseen in the video being shot from the front seat of a vehicle.

"It's just a helicopter, baby," her father said, a conflicting mix of reassurance and worry in his voice. "Keep recording, Jess."

"Okay, okay," a woman answered, her voice mostly breath.

Beyond the windshield, the helicopter lumbered off to the side of the road and swung sharply around, its nose pointed at the line of cars, the whole of it hanging there like some menacing insect.

"What's it—"

The woman never got the rest of the question out as the helicopter began to spit fire, a glowing jet of tracer rounds arcing over the line of cars. The woman screamed and the video jumped, just glimpses now showing the helicopter slipping back and forth, spraying fire from the cannon that hung beneath its nose like a misplaced stinger.

"Daddy!"

"Stay down!"

More quick flashes of the moment, recorded for whatever posterity mattered. The car lurched forward and bounced off the road, across the dirt median, turning fast and accelerating back toward Denver. The camera swung around now, shooting past a bawling child in the back seat, capturing the line of cars set afire, the helicopter laying a deadly carpet of shells along the roadway, cutting off any hope of escape from the city.

And then the video ended, and Jim Winters was back on screen, looking into the camera, quiet rage in his gaze, the cut of his jaw quivering slightly. He was gritting his teeth. Holding back. Crafting some measured commentary.

In the end he simply spoke more of the truth.

"Whatever happens," he began, "there can be no doubt after seeing what you just have that the government, our government, no longer represents the people. It no longer—"

A sharp hum interrupted Jim. He quieted and glanced upward, then behind, just in time to see the monitors that displayed the bright red rectangle still blocking other stations go dark. Then the space around him dimmed. Lights were going out. He turned and looked into the camera again, but said nothing as the feed from Network Five turned to static. All that remained of my connection to the outside world was electronic snow on the television.

For half an hour I sat and stared at the interference, waiting, hoping, even praying that the station would be back up. A simple power failure it could have been. Or...

Or, possibly, the fact that Network Five had broken through the Red Signal had piqued the interest of those pulling the strings. Men and women of power who watched as the rogue station broadcast what could not be allowed. What could not be disseminated.

Slaughter.

But it was worse than that, I thought. Maybe the station had been put out of commission by the government, but what it had shown, what had been recorded on the highway east of Denver, told more than just horror. More than sanctioned murder. Because I saw something in it that Jim Winters had not mentioned.

The helicopter strafing the road bore no markings. It had been painted solid black.

Eleven

I walked down my driveway to check the chain I'd secured across it and caught sight of something as I tugged on the sturdy barrier. Something through the trees. On the distant slopes, bolts of light from the setting sun painted the mountains as they did every day. But not like this.

A ten minute hike and climb up the hill to the south of my driveway brought me to the crest of the rise, the trees thinned naturally in one spot so I could stand and look across the valley to the peaks soon to be lost in shadow. For now they were still bathed in that warm glow from the fading day. A glow that usually set them alight with bursts of color, pines vibrant green, aspens glittering in what fall color they still retained this late in the season.

But I did not see that. What lay upon the mountains was a muted mask akin to cold granite, as if an avalanche of grey had swept down from the jagged tops more than halfway to the flats below. Wisps of color still remained low on the slopes, but above them to the crest of the peaks was little more than a colorless canvas, nature robbed of its beauty.

From my coat pocket I took the small pair of binoculars I always carried and brought them to my eyes, dialing in the distance as best I could with the compact optics. The view I found was more startling that what the naked eye had presented me.

It was death. Every tree and every bush in the dead zone was drained of their natural hues. They stood and squatted now as grey sentinels marching down the mountain toward the valley. Moving west. Coming my way.

I lowered the binoculars and stared at what was soon to be upon me. Yet it didn't make sense. A week before there'd been no sign of the blight across the valley. Now it had swept over and down the mountains, covering tens of miles in just days. How that was possible I didn't know, but possible it was. No, *certain* it was, because there was no denying what my own eyes were witness to.

"What the hell is this?" I asked the emptiness, but soon realized the land before me wasn't quite as empty as I'd thought. The rumbling engine beyond the trees below told me that.

I stowed my binoculars and moved quickly down the hill, driveway ahead, road to the right, though I could see neither through the still-green woods surrounding my refuge. My ears told me that the vehicle, the engine powering it having seen better days, was chugging along the road a few hundred yards to my east, heading north.

Until it slowed and turned. Moving slowly east. Up my driveway.

The AR swung easily from my shoulder as I brought it to bear, slowing my pace. I flipped the selector to fire and kept my finger against the side of the receiver, just above the trigger. Ahead, maybe fifty yards now, I could just make out the unnatural line cut through the forest—my driveway. And I could hear the vehicle chug to a stop, right about where my chain was. A door on the vehicle groaned open and then closed with a heavy thud.

Who the hell is out there? I asked myself. They'd taken the turn from the road to my driveway like they'd expected it. Like it was a known, not just some chance track off the way they were traveling. A half-dozen other driveways split off the road heading north to Whitefish, but the vehicle that now idled loudly some thirty yards from me had turned onto *mine*. With some purpose, it seemed.

Ten yards now, and I could make out the rough shape of small RV, not sleek and new, but boxy and well-traveled. A figure moved forward of it. Up my driveway. A man. He stepped over the chain that blocked his vehicle's path and continued.

Five yards now. I shifted left and skirted the edge of the driveway, keeping some cover of the woods between us. A sweatshirt covered his upper half, hood pulled over his head, hands jammed deep into the garment's from pockets. Just to keep warm, maybe.

Or gripping something within.

I raised the AR and stepped from the woods, taking a position in the middle of the driveway, lining the tactical sight on the hooded stranger, its illuminated reticle superimposing a glowing orange triangle on the man's back. At this distance I would not miss. That reality didn't make the possibility of having to do so any more palatable.

My finger eased onto the trigger, heart racing.

"Don't move," I said, and the stranger froze where he stood. "Take your hands out of your pockets. Slowly."

The man complied. His bare hands appeared, empty, and eased away from his body, fingers spread.

"Turn to face me," I ordered him.

He swiveled slowly, my finger drawing back from the trigger as his face came into view.

Twelve

"Eric," Marco said as he turned fully to face me.

I lowered my weapon but made no move toward my former employee. My friend. For a moment I simply stood there and studied him across the five yards that separated us. A thickening beard covered the lower half of his face—a face that had been perpetually smooth since I'd known him, shaved crisp and professional. Beneath the newly sprouted facial hair I could see that he was thinning, cheeks showing bone, eyes above them more pronounced, the slack skin forming hollows around them. The clothes he wore, utilitarian, layered for the weather, also could not hide a frame that was disappearing ounce by ounce.

It had been three weeks since I'd seen him. In another three there'd be nothing left of him to look at.

"Marco, what are you doing here?"

He glanced at the weapon in my hand. I swung it back over my shoulder and slung it, stepping toward him.

"We're heading south," he said, and looked past me, toward the front of the RV just visible past the chain.

We...

It hadn't occurred to me. His family. Judy and their son, Anthony. He was six. I glanced behind. Through the windshield of the RV could just make out two silhouettes, small one close to the larger, mother clutching her son. Their son.

"You were the only one I could think of who might..."

I looked back to Marco, a tide of embarrassment rising in him. Maybe cresting in shame. The look of a man who cannot see to his own. Cannot provide for them. Quiet desperation, I would even go as far as saying. Desperation edging toward defeat.

"You saw this all coming," Marco said. "You knew it was going down. You prepared. I wish I'd known. I wish you'd..."

He stopped there, never giving the accusation voice. But it deserved that.

"I wish I'd told you," I said. "There were reasons I couldn't. It involved someone else."

Marco nodded, piecing it together.

"The guy who showed up to see you."

"Yeah. If I'd said anything he would have been in danger."

"Isn't he in danger now like the rest of us?"

Marco had a point. But it didn't change things.

"Where are you heading down south?"

His hand slipped into his pocket and he pulled a folded piece of paper from it, opening the worn square, its edges frayed, creases tearing, as if he'd opened and closed the document again and again like some distant promise he had to convince himself of.

"Arizona," he said, pointing to a small map imprinted on the official-looking flyer, FEMA stamped at the top. "They have supplies there. Food and water and doctors."

I eyed the language in the instructions. *Relocation Centers... No Weapons... Martial Law...*

"Where did this come from? This paper?"

"There was a plane," Marco explained. "It flew over Missoula and dropped these everywhere."

A plane...

I'd heard an aircraft to the south earlier in the week, approaching Whitefish, it seemed, flying low and out of sight. I'd tried to zero in on it with my binoculars from the hill to the south of my refuge, but was never able to get a visual on it. Would the aircraft Marco had seen bothered to travel this far north, spreading leaflets to the wind in some effort reminiscent of psy-ops actions from wars past? Psychological operations, in this place and time, not to convince an enemy to surrender, but to herd a populace toward...

Toward what?

Then, another question rose—who was actually doing the herding?

Was it realistic to assume that some entity of the government still existed in a functioning capacity? I looked at the flyer again. It could have been printed by anyone with enough sense to paste a FEMA logo on it.

"Are you sure this is a good idea?" I asked Marco.

"I'm out of options, Eric. Everything is gone. Food, medicine, everything. The stores have been stripped since the first week. Hell, since the first days after..." His gaze dipped away again, that sense of failure gripping him. "That's why I'm here." He made himself look up, a light sheen spread across his eyes now. "I need food. Enough to get us down south."

Like most people, Marco had trusted that the government he'd paid for would be there in times like these. When a crisis arose to threaten the wellbeing of its citizens. He was learning how thin an implied covenant that had been.

"How long do you think it will take you to make it to Arizona?"

Marco thought for a moment, seemingly glad to focus on something beyond the helplessness he felt. "If the roads aren't too bad, three days. Maybe four. I had to stop a few times on the way up here to push some wrecks clear."

Four days. For a drive that would normally take one, if haste was the plan. Still, I thought he was being optimistic.

"Okay." I gestured toward the RV. "Wait with your family. I'll be right back."

He nodded a thanks, without knowing what help I would offer, and headed back toward the RV. I made my way up the driveway, equally at a loss. What would I do? Beyond what I *could* do?

I reached my house and went to the barn, unlocking it and swinging the door wide. Inside the aging structure I'd assembled a metal outdoor shed years ago, some place to securely store tools and supplies I left while immersed in sixty hour workweeks down in Missoula. Now it held not axes and shovels and chainsaws, but cases of MREs, my backup *backup* supply to augment what I kept in the house. I took six cases, a hundred and twenty individual meals, and loaded them onto the back of my ATV parked a few feet away. I hopped on sat with the engine off as I thought. As I questioned myself.

Was I really going to do this? Send my friend and his family on their way with enough food to last a week or so?

Stay alive...

Neil had told me that. Was I going to embrace that to the detriment of a friend I could help? And his family?

I fired up the ATV. Its engine struggled for a moment, then reached a familiar rhythm. The gas, even with stabilizers, wasn't degrading yet, but it would. Fuel didn't have an indefinite shelf life. Even the diesel stored in the trailer tank, which every week ran automatically through the filter system I'd pieced together, wouldn't last forever. Eventually enough moisture would collect in it, too much for the slowly wearing filter to process, and then any use of the generator, or my truck, would come to an end. Just as everything else would.

Even my friend and his family.

I rode out of the barn and down the driveway, stopping at the chain, Marco waiting there, his wife and son in the cab of the RV, looking out. She smiled at me, that kind of expression that offered thanks and fear at the same instant. "Thank you, man," Marco said, seeing the boxes on the back of the ATV. He stepped over the chain as I climbed off the four-wheeler. "I'll never be able to pay you back."

"Listen," I said, hesitating for an instant, though I'd already made the decision.

"What?"

I looked to the faces beyond the windshield, then to Marco. My friend.

"Stay," I told him. "I've got room, enough food to keep all of us going for a year if we're careful. That's not counting what we can add by hunting. Even scavenging if it comes to that."

My friend stared at me, smiling as tears threatened. Gratitude at my offer. My gesture of humanity. Then he smiled and shook his head.

"We can't. Anthony needs doctors. They say there are doctors in Arizona."

Then I remembered. The boy, barely past kindergarten, was already facing a life of medical procedures for a heart condition. Medicine had kept the affliction in check, but surgery was the only way to deal with it in the long run. And that would never happen here.

I also worried that it would never happen where they were heading.

"Marco, what if there's nothing there? What if you get there and whatever FEMA was planning is just overwhelmed? Their track record isn't the best in major disasters, and this is way beyond some hurricane or earthquake. This is biblical. How can they handle thousands, maybe millions of people who all need every basic need provided? Not to mention what you need for Anthony?"

He listened to what I said, then nodded, that sheen on his eyes thickening. Tears threatening.

"It's the only hope there is," Marco said. "If we stay here he dies. His medicine is almost gone as it is. Every pharmacy has been looted. Hospitals are abandoned. I have to believe that there's help down south. I have to."

And that was it. I knew he was right. Just as Neil could not abandon his father to seek survival with me, Marco could not turn his back on the chance of keeping his son alive. No father could. I could have told him of the terrible reports I'd seen from Denver several weeks back, implying that routes to the south were likely to be beyond dangerous. But nothing I could say would convince him, so I didn't try.

I helped him load the cases of MREs and said a final goodbye. A very final goodbye, I feared. With me guiding him, Marco backed the RV down the cramped gravel driveway and onto the road, swinging it around and heading south.

Thirteen

A single car sped past as I worked where my driveway spilled onto the road, heading south with some haste, ignoring the sight of me, standing on the dirt shoulder, pick axe in hand. It was either a skittish Canadian, or one of the few holdouts up near Eureka who'd given up hope of any government help reaching this far north as winter bore down. Possibly they were aiming for Arizona, as Marco was. He'd left the day before, hoping that the promised assistance was real. That the flyers drifting from the sky were akin to messages from heaven. True offers of salvation.

I believed in hope. But not fairy tales. Many of the people moving south would, likely soon, turn tail and head back for familiar ground—if the FEMA promises that were supposed to exist in Arizona were as hollow as I feared they would turn out to be. The people who'd aimed themselves at that spot on the map, clinging to hope, might find nothing different than what they'd left. Hunger. Maybe starvation. They'd be desperate. If they did travel this road on any return trip, if *anyone* did, I wanted them to move right past the spot where I stood, with no hint that any access to my property had ever been here.

For six hours that's what I'd worked at, hauling tools from my truck parked out of sight up the driveway, tearing up the graded connection between driveway and road, pick axe chipping into the first twenty yards of the narrow path. I chopped holes in the cold ground and rolled jagged mini-boulders into them. What deadfall that had already accumulated as fall ticked toward its end I spread about. As darkness spilled like black water over the eastern peaks I set my chainsaw to screaming, blade cutting into old trees to either side of the mangled driveway, felling a full dozen of the fifty footers so they lay across the hidden way. In the spring they would begin to rot. By next fall there would be no discernable hint that a driveway had been here, just a tangle of fallen pines and weathered rocks to match the scenery along the miles of roadway north and south of my refuge.

This did not mean, though, that I was locking myself in. Prior to erasing the obvious connection between my refuge and whatever would survive of civilization, I'd widened an old hiking path that ran from behind my barn along the base of the hill and followed the stream to the road. With careful driving, and maintenance of the makeshift driveway, I could leave and reenter my refuge some three hundred yards down the road, emerging from the trees like a lumbering bison might.

Finished, I loaded the last of the tools into my pickup and reached for the driver's door, ready to climb in. But I didn't. I stopped. Sensing something. Out there. In the woods.

I came around the front of my truck and let my right hand rest atop the pistol on my hip as I stood there. Listening. Looking.

The last wisps of daylight drizzled through the canopy, cutting the din hardly at all. It was a world of shadows out there between the ranks of trees marching up the slope. I wished at that moment that I'd brought along my AR topped with a night vision scope. But all I had with me were my senses. And my wits. The former were telling me there was nothing visible or audible out there. The latter, though, was offering a different interpretation. A gut feeling that I was being watched.

By what, I had no idea.

I reached to the small holder on my belt exactly opposite my weapon's holster, withdrawing the flashlight secured within. Bringing it up I clicked it on and sprayed two-hundred lumens into the woods, sweeping the harsh white beam slowly left, then right, tracking it back and forth up the slope beyond, as if following some imagined switchback trail. It revealed nothing.

That didn't mean I was alone.

The beam went dark with another click of the switch. I finally climbed into my truck and drove slowly up what remained of my driveway, glancing out the side windows, and to the rearview, continuously, unable to shake the feeling that I had company.

* * *

The sensation stayed with me through the evening.

I wandered through the house, taking care of chores. Sweeping. Wiping down the bathroom sink. Dusting. But still I felt it, that someone had been out there, watching. And that they still were.

Each time, before leaving a room, I'd close the door for a moment, stopping light from the great room from filtering in down the hall. I'd stand near the window and look out into the dark woods, letting my eyes adjust, small details resolving, movement registering.

Animals. Branches shifting in the wind. That's all I saw from all four sides of the house. Relative emptiness spilling from the forest. I was alone.

But I didn't feel that way.

I needed to do something, I realized. Not now in the dark, but in the morning. I couldn't finish it then, but I could begin. Days it would take, most likely, but at least I'd anticipated having to consider such an endeavor, and had, on one of my shopping sprees prior to the Red Signal, secured all the equipment necessary to alleviate my concern of being observed.

When the sun rose, I would set about turning the tables on whoever was out there.

Fourteen

It took three days.

I was exhausted, and sore, and thoroughly satisfied with my ability to turn a few thousand feet of wire and some robust electronics into a high-tech version of a bells tied to a trip wire.

In my great room, mounted to the wall to the left of the hearth, was what I began to think of as Intruder Central, a panel of warning lights connected to two roughly concentric rings of sensors surrounding my refuge. Placed at two-hundred and three-hundred feet from my front door, the layers of motion and thermal sensors would, if my planning and execution was correct, give me advance notice of anyone approaching. Or anything. That would take some fine tuning, so that scurrying critters did not set the amber and red lights to blinking every five minutes.

That wasn't my only concern with the system. There was the power consideration. Juicing up dozens and dozens of sensors over nearly a mile of wire was going to tax the already stringent energy budget I'd made for myself. My solution was to energize the sensors only fifty percent of the time, ten minutes on and ten off, in a random pattern that would leave a good portion of the perimeter covered at any one time. In addition to that, only the thermal sensors would be active after dark, these easily adjustable to ignore anything but the heat signature of a man or larger.

Secured in trees and strategically buried in shallow holes dug in the earth, the electronic eyes and ears would let me know just how real my feeling of being watched was.

* * *

I didn't have to wait long. Eighteen hours, in fact. The day after the system was complete, as the clock ticked toward midnight, an amber light began flashing, indicating a heat sensor to the north was picking up something.

Or someone.

The electronic beeping that announced the possible intrusion in concert with the light would have woken me had I been asleep. But I wasn't. I'd turned on the television for a few minutes, just to see if the Denver station was still lost in static. It was, and as I was turning the television off, the sharp chirping sounded. I stood and stared at the panel.

Until another sensor tripped. This one connected to the inner ring. Whatever was out there was coming my way.

I quickly grabbed my AR topped with the night vision scope and doused the lights in the house. Just a flicker from the fire dying in the hearth struggled to light the great room as I moved to the front door and stepped out onto the east-facing porch. Whatever was approaching was off to my left. I came off the porch and crept slowly along the front of the house, stopping at the corner so that the whole expanse of the north side was visible, along with the dark woods beyond. Taking a knee I steadied my AR and began to scan the landscape, the artificial illumination provide by the optics piercing the night that hung thick between the trees. And nothing more.

Either my system had gone haywire, or whatever had tripped it was hanging back, watching, waiting, alerted to my presence. Perhaps the front door had slapped shut a bit too loud behind me. Or the light of the dying fire might have silhouetted me just enough. If either were true, it would likely behoove me to stop referring to the presence in the woods as a 'what', and fully embrace that it was a 'who'. And if they were alerted to me, I damn sure wanted them to know at this point that I was just as much in the know as to their presence.

"Your best move would be to leave!"

I shouted the warning and waited. Maybe not for any reply, but for some sound of retreat. A hurried scramble through the woods.

But I heard nothing. I saw nothing.

"I know you're out there. You are on my land. I'm prepared to defend it."

For an instant I considered firing off a single shot to punctuate my seriousness. The realization that doing so might bring return fire left that idea dying before execution. I kept scanning the woods as I stilled myself, not moving from the spot for ten full minutes. Finally I backed away from the corner of the house and returned inside, closing the door, every action measured, staying as quiet as I could as I returned to Intruder Central.

Every warning light was now dark.

I knew I could not be the only one in these woods. Other properties dotted the forested landscape from Whitefish to the Canadian border. But in all my time visiting my refuge, when wariness and security were thoughts far from my mind, and presumably others', I'd come across just two or three people while out fishing the streams, or stalking deer. But never while lounging on the porch. No person had wandered past on a day hike. Without being alone, I'd always felt alone.

Until now.

But the intruder had heeded the warnings I'd shouted into the night. They were gone. Or gone from where my sensors could monitor their presence.

Gone, though, might only be a temporary situation. Evidence, from gut feelings to the repaired valve on my propane tank, abounded that they, or someone, had come before. I had to expect they would again.

Still, though, what motive they had for being near and not making themselves known eluded my understanding. A myriad of reasons were possible. Some quite unpleasant.

I lit the fire in the stove in my bedroom and settled in for the night. My AR rested close to my bed. Closer than the night before.

Fifteen

Five weeks after the Red Signal I woke to what I thought was fog swirling beyond my bedroom window. Wind had whipped all night, buffeting the house. I imagined the mist was dragged over the hills by the blow, but a moment's thought on that as I stood next to the bed chased that possibility from the realm of reality. What was being dragged past my window, thick and grey, was coming from the east, opposite the usual prevailing winds. More than that, though, was what I saw stuck to the outside of the pane as I approached. Not just some dewy collection on the glass, but a thickening, pasty smear hued halfway between black and white. Something akin to ash. But I smelled no smoke.

I dressed and headed to the front door, slinging my AR as I stepped out into a world whose color had been washed away. Every tree I could make out through the grainy mist was slathered in the grey dust. My pickup was coated, its already silvery paint lost beneath the scummy grit.

It was the blight. The spawn of it. Death from the trees and growth already afflicted across the valley, spread now not by gentle breezes or on the feet of creatures that scurried on the earth of sailed above it, but by shifting winds, dragging the inevitable west. I wondered how long it would be before the trees that surrounded my refuge, *my* trees, were afflicted, turning to dried grey sentinels that would harbor no life. That would stand like gangly beasts with wasted limbs stretched out, naked, against the sky.

Soon, I feared. Soon the death that was across the valley, that was spread upon the earth, would settle upon my place.

The filmy cloud drifting from the sky swept over my exposed skin and clung to my clothes. I swatted at my shoulders to knock it away, but more found its way to me. Even into me, every breath fouled by it. It grated at my throat, and soon I was coughing and spitting gobs of mucus that came out looking like flecks of wet concrete. After just a few minutes I could take it no more and retreated, shedding my top layer of clothing just inside the front door. It piled atop the old wood floor, grey dust billowing.

"Dammit," I swore mildly, the mess wafting all around me.

But my annoyance at the scene inside faded as I went to the window and looked through a patch on the glass not yet smudged by the detritus swirling in from the east. The world was wasting grey. And pieces of that world, this new world, had come in on me. I brought the fingertips of one hand to my nose and sampled the scent. There was none. The foul, fine grit was anonymous.

"Shit!"

In a building panic, I swatted the remaining dust from my hands, then my arms, remnants clinging, a layer of the stuff seeming embedded in and on my skin. I shed the remainder of my clothes and ran, naked, to the bathroom, cranking the shower on to full, ignoring the icy blast jetting from the head. There'd been no time to turn the water heater on and let it come to a tolerable temperature, so what hit me as I jumped beneath the spray shocked me to the bone. I screamed out in actual pain as the near freezing water, drawn directly from the pond, was forced over my filthy body by the pump whose whirring motor was drowned out by my cry. I scrubbed and scraped and scratched, trying to rub the blight from my skin. It had worked its way into every wrinkle, every fold, every crevice.

After ten minutes I turned the shower off and wrapped a towel around my shivering body. I had taken care of the outside.

But the acrid dust still grated within, in my throat, my lungs. I went to the sink and nearly jerked the cap from the bottle of mouthwash, pouring it straight into my mouth, gargling and spitting, again and again until the forced retching turned real and vomit spewed into the old porcelain bowl. Twice more the contents of my stomach spilled out before the spasms I'd brought on subsided.

Catching my breath, I straightened and looked at myself in the mirror above the sink. The whole of my body still shook from the cold, but I was clean. I'd gotten the scummy residue of the blight off of me, and, hopefully, out of me. I knew I'd panicked and reacted irrationally, with haste, and I couldn't afford to behave that way. There'd been no indication before the Red Signal, from any sources, that the blight could affect a person directly. It was not poison. It was not an infectious agent to humans. Contact with it was, almost certainly, little more than an annoyance.

Still, I wanted it off of me and out of me.

I calmed and dried off, dressing in clean clothes and building the fire in the hearth to a raging blaze. As it warmed me I looked to the television and powered it up for a moment. Static still filled the screen, and I turned it quickly off, wanting no reminder right then that the world beyond my refuge was gone. Made mute.

Or, maybe, that was the best way to think of it. All that could have happened to the people 'out there' had already come to pass. The deed was done. What food there might have been in storage was gone for weeks now. Bodies had withered. Weakened masses would have succumbed to disease. For certain it was possible that large numbers were still hanging on, but what were they going through?

That was where my embrace of silence settled me. Their screams had been quieted, or soon would be, I told myself. Marco. His family. All at peace, or nearing that state of finality.

Neil among them.

This was the hardest to believe. Neil would have tended to his father, as he told me, but he would also had fought to survive. For the both of them. Scrounged to keep him and his loved one going. You could drop a thousand people in the middle of the ocean and Neil would be the last one treading water.

So it was hard to imagine him as gone. But it was also the best bit of mental magic I could play with. His suffering was over.

I began to wonder when mine would begin.

Sixteen

Winter came with flurries in the dark and the muffled crack of distant rifle shots. Not a hunter out to supplement their larder, I was certain, the repeated volleys echoing from diverse origins indicating that not only was someone shooting—someone else was shooting back.

I slipped into my cold weather camo and grabbed my AR-15, tactical scope atop it. In no way was I planning on joining whatever fray was underway, but I did want a better vantage away from my house to zero in on the sound. Leaving through the front door after killing the lights within, I moved across the driveway, just a skim of snow crunching beneath my boots and dusting my pickup, the grey grit of the blight's arrival three days ago washed away by rain the following morning. Rain that had chilled and crystallized in a blast of arctic air sweeping down from Canada.

As I slipped into the woods and began to skirt the low edge of the hill between my house and the road the volume of fire picked up. This was not just a simple exchange of shots—this was a firefight.

Reaching the edge of the hill I could just make out the road a hundred yards distant, ribbon of asphalt disappearing under the falling snow, just a hint of moonlight filtering through the thin storm above. But there was light, in small pulses, bursting beyond the hills this side of the road's junction with the highway. Three miles to the south, it would appear, cracks following each series of flashes after a few seconds, sound of the fight catching up with what was visible. There were no houses in that exact spot. No buildings of any kind. Whitefish was further south, still. Yet out there some conflict had arisen, between parties unknown.

I needed to know who was out there. Who was engaged in the battle in my figurative backyard? Were they just bands of survivors skirmishing? Or some larger group? Military, perhaps? And, most important to me, were they moving this way?

Ten minutes it took me, traveling cautiously, planning every step, trying to avoid a stumbling mishap in the dark, until I finally reached the forward slope where the landscape opened in front of me. Where before there had been just flashes bulging beyond the crest of the hill, now there were sharp white flares, muzzles of weapons spitting fire. A dozen or more on the east, firing west, and less than half that to the west returning fire, the diminishing rate from the right indicating who was taking heavier casualties.

But who the hell were they? Either side?

Confident that I was concealed by both night and the forest, whose supple limbs and green foliage had begun to dry and droop, I advanced further, and faster, skirting the road heading south, close enough to be seen were anyone looking. None were, I was certain. Anyone who might be in the vicinity, a doubtful proposition at best, would be focused on the battle raging just to the south. Still, I wished I'd grabbed the AR fitted with the night vision scope, which would have given me a bit more ability for stand-off observation. As it was, I had to get closer if I wanted to discern the who and what of what was happening.

BAM! BAM BAM BAM!

Without warning the fire shifted, less than half a mile south now, rounds from the battle splintering trees above and around me. I hit the dirt and rolled behind the stout trunk of a pine as the errant shots peppered the area. There was no chance that I was being targeted. My position was simply in the background as the firefight moved, the smaller force maneuvering for position, or attempting to flee.

I rolled carefully to peer past the tree and brought my AR to bear. Not to join the fray, but to use its optics for observation. The simple 4 power scope, with its illuminated reticle and wide field of vision didn't bring much additional clarity. But it brought enough as the fire suddenly died.

Lights came on as I looked through my tactical scope. Distant beams sweeping the landscape. Small. Like handheld flashlights, or similar affixed to weapons. The narrow cones of brightness they spread revealed nothing about those who wielded them, but made clear why the fire had stopped.

Body after body was lit up. Members of the vanquished force, it had to be. Men, or women, crouched near each and stripped the fallen of weapons and supplies, then used long knives to cut across the throat of each. A silent *coup de grace*. No need to waste a bullet should one near death need to be dispatched. What I was witness to was quiet and quick. Intimately brutal. And telling.

Sides had been chosen in some conflict, I knew. Over what, I didn't. Food, most likely, though, understanding the nature of man, that could have been secondary to many things. Land. Water. Power. Or simple control.

It was hardly a month since the Red Signal and already humanity was devolving into tribes. Or new tribes, I should say. We'd always separated ourselves, by border, race, religion. Even when we'd attempted to erase those divisions, ghosts of them remained. Finding old fault lines, or creating new ones, was well within our capacity.

For a while I lay still and observed, trying to glean as much information from what I could see. Gathering intelligence, I supposed it was, though whether I was collecting such on friend or foe I could not tell. I did know, though, that until I possessed some certainty as to the victors' motives, I wanted to steer well clear of them.

After fifteen minutes of watching, the majority of their lights went dark, just a few remaining as they moved south, lost in the night as they traveled toward Whitefish. Whether that was their destination, or just a point on the map to be transited on their way to wherever they were going, I could only surmise. I was simply glad they were gone.

I rose and made my way back to my refuge. At the front door I paused, hearing something beyond. A familiar sound.

Beeping.

Quickly I entered and went straight for the alarm panel, expecting to see a flashing light matched to the audible warning. But there was none.

My pulse raced. I locked the front door and moved through the house, checking every window and door, pistol in hand, eyes tuned to the darkness within. To say I was unsettled was an understatement. The alarm signal cutting out just as I returned home meant one of two things, I knew. I had been tracked by my visitor as I returned from watching the firefight, and they had broken away just as I reached the house—or they did not break away, and they were inside my perimeter where the sensors would not detect them. Anywhere out to fifty yards from the house. From me.

Watching.

Seventeen

What had fallen the previous week hadn't stuck, winter dragging its feet so that the minor accumulation of snow remained as nothing more than slushy puddles and shallow bogs of mud. But real winter would come, and before that white misery arrived I needed to do what I should have right after arriving. I'd purchased all that was necessary to do so in the weeks before the Red Signal, trucking the implements up alongside other supplies.

The ladder leaned against the north side of the barn, giving me access to the sketchy section of roof some twenty feet above the cold, hard earth. 'Hard' being the operative word. Falling from height here, almost any height, would lay a hurt on me that would certainly reap more than simple bruises. I needed to be careful.

But I also needed to get the spongy patch of roofing replaced. Already I'd braced the structure from within. Peeling back the flimsy shingles that covered the area and replacing them was all that remained to give my barn the ability to survive yet another winter. Beyond that, I could make no guarantees.

As I worked I would pause every ten or fifteen minutes and scan the dying woods that surrounded me. Dead, mostly now, the process complete. The blight had laid claim to the north of the state, it seemed. To the whole of the planet, I suspected. But I was not looking out upon the thinning grey landscape for appraisal purposes. I was looking for my visitor.

They'd come again two nights earlier. Probing my outermost ring of sensors without advancing further. I was suspecting they'd discovered I was aware of their presence. It could be that they were testing my defenses, if you could call it that. I didn't want to. Their motive, as yet, was a mystery to me.

Focusing again on the repairs to be made, I drew the hammer back and swung it again and again, driving nails through the shingles, the repair proceeding uneventfully until I missed my mark, the hard steel head of the tool striking the edge of a loose bit of bracing. The foot-long piece of wood was launched upward, spinning its rough edge toward my face. I ducked and turned away, the length of lumber sailing past and thudding across the roof deck, tumbling over the edge and disappearing almost silently into the slushy earth below.

My heart raced for an instant, from the abruptness of the near miss. But as it stilled, and I calmed, a more worrying realization rose—I could have been hurt. *Actually* hurt. Not from some fall off the roof that could kill me, but from a simple gash laid by dirtied wood, some infection possible, if not likely.

I was not prepared for that. I'd gathered all types of medical supplies. From bandages to makeshift splints. I could even suture a wound too large to be bandaged. Every conceivable over-the-counter medication was in my first aid kit. I had everything anyone might need.

All but antibiotics.

It had simply never occurred to me that I would need any back when I could have cajoled a prescription out of my doctor. Now, with a fraction of an inch separating me from a wound which could have brought on infection, I knew I'd screwed up. And I had to correct that. Doing so meant one thing.

I'd have to venture into civilization.

Eighteen

I saw the bone on the sidewalk near the alcove of the flower shop. It was long and buttery in color, picked clean of flesh, and lay near the blackened stubs of burnt down logs. A few cinderblocks had been placed around the makeshift fire to create a windbreak. There was no one in sight, and no sound but the stiff breeze rushing past me, tossing trash and twigs, whistling as it washed through the metal frames of store awnings stripped of their fabric. For a moment I stood still, finger nearer the trigger of my AR than a moment earlier, sampling the silence that whispered through downtown Eureka, a scant few miles from the Canadian border. I was waiting for any sign that the person, or people, who'd been here still lurked in the area. When I was satisfied that I was alone I focused on the bone and convinced myself that my first instinct, my first fear, had been correct.

It was a human bone. The long bone from the leg. The thigh. One of the meatiest parts of a human being, thick with flesh and muscle. All of that was gone here. My mind tried to use words like 'missing' or 'taken', when what I knew to be true was that the meat had been cooked down and picked off this bone over the fire that had been here.

Picked and eaten.

That part of the new existence had begun. Cannibalism. It did not surprise me that such a thing would come to be, but still the fact that man had the capacity to feast upon his fellow man when the need arose brought a chill to me. One deeper than what the weather lay upon my skin.

But even the horror of seeing what I was confirmed one fact, uplifting in a small way—there were others. People still trying to survive. Men, women, maybe children hanging on. If just barely.

I left the sight behind and entered the front of *Keeping It Reel*, the fishing store that Keith Markey ran when the world was whole and filled with sound, and smiles, and the scent of cool green days. Not the thick stench of decay. The front door had been broken in, windows smashed. Display cases lay toppled on the floor. Their contents, what hadn't been looted, was scattered across the space, from entry to the register counter. That device itself, which once held cash and spat receipts, was upended, its drawer open and empty. Someone, at some point, had decided that, despite the chaos enveloping civilization as a whole, having a pocketful of tens and twenties was a decent idea. Perhaps it was their bone cooked to black I'd seen outside.

I moved past the counter, stepping over more merchandise, broken and discarded, and passed the once pristine tanks that Keith had tended with such care. Tropical fish once swam in the bubbling waters. Now, just a single slender carcass floated atop the putrid water, the rest having become food for the last survivor. The need, if not the desire, to eat one another crossed species, it seemed.

Beyond the tanks were a wall of shelves still relatively intact, though every item upon them was tossed about the floor below. I slung my AR and crouched, sifting through the debris, separating out plastic bottles, scanning each one. It was a running joke that Keith Markey ran a store where you could buy the implements to gut a fish, or to mend another's infected fin. His philosophy, he once shared with me, was that you ate trout, and admired most everything else through glass. Beyond the tanks was where one would find the implements to aid them in the latter endeavor. And where I hoped to find a certain antibiotic designed to treat diseases that fish suffered, and which just happened to be chemically identical to specific antibiotics prescribed for humans.

I'd realized that seeking the same medication in a pharmacy would be pointless. They would have been cleaned out weeks ago, looted to the rafters. Just as the larger and more well-stocked stores in Whitefish certainly were. For the moment, though, traveling there was out of the question. This I'd decided after witnessing the firefight and its aftermath between my refuge and Whitefish. North to Eureka was the only choice I had, the only choice I'd given myself, and it was where, finally, I struck pay dirt.

Bright yellow bottles of the aquatic antibiotic lay in a heap beneath a collection of aquarium decorations. I pushed the packages of faux treasure chests and miniature deep sea divers clear and scooped every bottle I could find into the cargo pockets of my pants, seven in all, more than enough, I hoped, for any potential injury requiring a course of antibiotics to treat. Finished, I came around the toppled shelves at the back of the store and turned toward the front door.

That's when I saw the boy.

He stood just outside the shattered front door, on the sidewalk, staring in at me, remarkably bright eyes over thin cheeks. A quick appraisal of his stature set his age at about nine, likely no older. In his hand a candy bar of some sort was held in a death grip, upper portion of its wrapper peeled back, exposing the sweet, dark candy within. A smear of the treat darkened the skin around his lips. For a few seconds we just looked at each other. There was no fear in his eyes, just surprise.

"Hello," I said.

"Hello yourself," a woman behind me said, at the same instant I felt the round chill of a rifle barrel touch the base of my skull.

I didn't dare turn. Without prompting I eased my hands from the AR slung across my chest.

"I'm not going to hurt you," I said, and the rifle barrel jabbed hard against my skull, pushing my head forward.

"I will damn sure hurt you before you get the chance to do anything to us."

She sounded something beyond desperate. Determined. Maybe committed. To what, I wasn't certain. The boy, maybe.

"Your son?" I asked.

"Don't concern yourself with us," the woman said. "Do you have any food?"

"A little. In my right cargo pocket. Just some energy bars."

I sensed the woman crouching behind, rifle still in contact with the back of my head, from a lower angle now. She reached to the pocket just above my right knee and probed it. Her hand came out with just what I'd described and she stood again in my blind spot. My gaze angled toward the boy once more. He had the chocolate bar to his mouth and was chewing slowly on a piece he'd just bitten off. The energy bars sailed past me and landed near the boy's feet.

"Take those," the woman instructed. "Put them in your pockets."

"Do you have any more?" the woman pressed. "Anywhere?"

"I can get you some," I told her, and again the rifle barrel jabbed against the bony flesh at the back of my head.

"Where is it?!"

This was beyond committed, I realized.

"WHERE IS THE FOOD?!!!"

I felt the weapon shudder in her grip. My deepest hope right then was that her finger was off the trigger.

"You're not the only one afraid," I said. She quieted. Fast breaths filled the space between us. "I'm afraid, too."

"I'm not..."

She wasn't professing any lack of fear. No, what she'd said was preface to more. To some statement relevant to the situation, be it the standoff between us, or the larger apocalypse that had befallen the world. Whatever it was, I decided to chance a move. To interject some understanding into the softening of her demeanor. Slowly, I began to turn, just my head at first, then the whole of my body. The rifle barrel came away from my skull and I felt the woman backing away before my gaze finally settled on her.

"You're not what?"

It was a simple question I proposed. Just something to elicit some response as I appraised who I faced. She was in her early thirties and pretty, even with the folds of skin that had appeared on her face where muscle and fat had once given contour to her appearance. There was a clear resemblance between her and the boy, in the eyes, more their shape than any similar coloring. He had thinned, but nowhere as much as the woman had. Clearly she'd been diverting sustenance to him, to her own detriment.

This was a mother's love I was witnessing.

"You're not what?" I repeated calmly.

For a moment she did as I had, took in the sight of me, then nodded toward the front of the store where her son stood, lever action 30-30 in her hands shifting in concert with the gesture.

"I'm not letting us turn into what's out there."

Out there. It took little imagination to understand what she was referring to. Or who.

Cannibals.

"I need food," she said, then quickly added, "For him."

She spoke as though seeking food for herself was selfish.

A mother's love...

"Are you from Eureka?" I asked.

She shook her head quickly.

"Canada?"

Another head shake, less forceful this time.

"Do you want to tell me where you're fr—"

"Where is the food?" she asked again, some low menace in her voice now. Her finger flexed on the old lever action's trigger.

"Where are you from?" I pressed calmly.

Still she didn't answer.

"Whitefish," the answer came, from behind, the boy speaking. I glanced back to him. He took another bite of chocolate and slowly chewed it as he eyed me.

"There's no food there," the woman said. "We can't go back there."

I nodded, thinking. The reality was that I still had to, somehow, get this woman to a point of calm that we could converse without firearms being involved. Reiterating an offer I'd made a moment before might open the door to that possibility.

"I do have food," I said. "I can bring you some."

She half smiled, but didn't lower the rifle an inch.

"Yeah, you head off and leave us and we never see you again."

"Yeah," I said, concurring with what she was surmising. "I could do that. But what good does keeping me here do if you're not going to end up like the cannibals?"

What I'd just told her sank in, slowly, and finally her weapon did come down, its muzzle pointed at the ravaged floor.

"What's your name?" I asked.

"I'm Sarah Elway."

"I'm Jeff," the boy said, slipping past to join his mother, who pulled him into a tired, one-handed hug against her hip.

I slid the AR slung across my chest under my left arm so that it hung behind me now. Sarah placed her lever action atop a dirty counter and groped at the edge for support. She was weak. Far weaker than I'd suspected. Her knees buckled and both her son and I grabbed her, setting gently down, back against an empty display stand.

"Give me one of those bars," I told Jeff, and he reached into his pocket.

"No!" Sarah said sharply. "Those are for him."

I took the energy bar from the boy and peeled the wrapper back, then twisted a bit from one end and held it out to Sarah.

"Eat this."

She shook her head at my direction.

"Look, if you want him to eat, you're going to need to eat." I eased the piece of food closer to her. "He needs you."

That seemed to register. Not that she'd never thought or accepted that, but to hear another lay it out, with the circumstances plain as day, was enough that she reached up and took what I was offering and slipped it into her mouth. She chewed, her eyes closing, as if some silent prayer had gripped her. Tears trickled from her eyes as they opened again and looked to me.

"I'm sorry," she said.

"For what? Putting a gun to my head? I've had worse happen on dates."

She smiled at my attempt at humor, then took the rest of the bar from me and bit off another piece. As she held it I saw the simple diamond ring on the third finger of her left hand.

"Where is your husband?"

I knew it was a risk to ask. Especially in front of her son. Had some horror befallen him? Was that the reason for his absence from their immediate lives?

"He's in the Navy," Sarah answered, a distant hope to the way she said it. Some true likelihood that, whatever they were faced with, he was alive.

"We're going to meet him," Jeff said. "In Washington."

Sarah smiled at her son and nodded, the gesture filled with pained hope. But hope nonetheless.

"Bremerton," she said. "He's on a submarine. We haven't heard from him since before..."

"Because they can't always send messages," Jeff added quickly, wanting to counter any negativity implied by his mother. "They have to stay hidden underwater."

"That's true," I told the boy. "I've heard that." I looked back to Sarah. "Seems to me a pretty safe place to be is on a sub under the ocean right now."

She accepted that assurance with a nod and a smile and kept eating, her son slipping even closer to his mother, curling up against her on the dirty floor. They were a pair. A team. Alone in what had become a built-up wilderness.

Alone...

The idea came to me naturally. I'd made the same offer to Marco. Sarah Elway and her boy, Jeff, needed help. Needed a chance to get through this nightmare. I was well stocked. If nothing else I could give them a chance to get healthy and ready for any trek to the Pacific Northwest.

"Listen, I have food, and plenty of room. It's safe. You can both come rest up at my place. It's not that far south of here."

Sarah had seemed to listen with openness, until I mentioned the direction of my refuge. She shook her emphatically after that.

"No. We're not going south. We have to head north, and then west."

"You can still do that," I assured her. "Just after you—"

"No," she said, with quiet force. "There's not a chance in hell we're moving one inch to the south."

Jeff nodded agreement with his mother. Total agreement.

"That's where the Major is."

I looked between mother and son, puzzled.

"Who?"

"The Major," Jeff repeated, then he clammed up, seeming to want to visit the subject no more. He tucked his head in against his mother's shoulder.

"You're from south of here and you haven't had any run-in with him?"

I shook my head at Sarah's question.

"I'm north of Whitefish."

"Well, my advice is, don't go south."

Her words were more warning than suggestion. I wondered if the firefight I'd watched between my refuge and Whitefish had any relation to what might be motivating her fear of the area.

"Who is this Major?"

"That's what he calls himself," Sarah explained. "And what his people call him. Major James Layton."

"Is he in uniform?"

She shook her head at my question.

"He came into town three weeks after everything went to hell."

"After the Red Signal?" I asked, the timing worrisome. That would have been about the time Marco was heading south from my refuge with his family.

"Yeah," she confirmed, finishing the last of the energy bar, a bitter exasperation rising. "That damn thing blocked everything. I couldn't get in touch with Charlie's—that's my husband—with his base in Bremerton. I just wanted to see if they knew anything. No one could get through to anyone, anywhere, I think."

"The police were able to get some radio traffic through," I told her. "So some allowance for official communication was made."

"Official," she said, nearly spitting a laugh after the word. "The 'official' people in Whitefish didn't seem to stick around to do much communicating. After the third day, I didn't see a cop or firefighter anywhere in town. But I tried not to go out too much after that."

"Dangerous?"

"A lot of shooting. Fires. By the end of the first week it was chaos. People were killing each other for whatever food they had in their cupboards. All the stores had been cleaned out in the first few days. I was lucky that my husband made a big deal about being prepared. He grew up in the Midwest with a lot of ice storms. No power, no open stores."

"So you had food," I said.

"For a while. Until I traded it away."

"For what?" I asked, unsure what would be worth more than the thing keeping them alive.

"Freedom," she answered. That, too, was a precious commodity, often taken for granted. "When the Major arrived with his people, he started gathering all the supplies to keep under guard. He was some kind of authority figure."

"With sufficient weaponry, I imagine."

She nodded.

"No one was in control," she went on. "People weren't even able to control themselves. The few who'd survived, who'd hung on, they gave in. By that time they wanted someone to take charge."

"You didn't," I said.

"My parents escaped from East Germany when there still was an East Germany," she explained. "I was born here, in America, but they made sure I knew what kind of system they'd lived under. One thing they drilled into me was that you never, ever, allow yourself to live under someone else's control. No matter what sort of order or utopia they promise."

"Freedom isn't free," I said, and she nodded.

"So I bribed my way out with what was left of our food." She gave a small, light chuckle. "You don't have to be a big country like East Germany to have graft and bribery be the way things get done."

"You made your way up here after that?"

"Yeah. We couldn't head down toward Kalispell. The Major was telling people that he was securing that as well."

"He didn't give any indication where he was from? Anything?"

"No. Just rolled into town with thirty, maybe forty people, all armed to the teeth, and took over." Sarah quieted, thinking back. "Not everyone gave in. Not everyone had the ability to bribe their way out."

Some memory was rising. A terrible memory, I could tell.

"That bad?"

She didn't nod this time. Didn't respond at all for a moment.

"He told people if they tried to leave, they'd die. My friend, Ellen, she told the Major's men that she had a cabin she wanted to go to, but they wouldn't let her leave town. They said if she tried, she'd be killed."

She was spinning a harsh tale. So harsh I hoped it was at least partly embellished.

"I won't go south again," she said. "You shouldn't either. Not that far. Stay away from Whitefish."

Some trauma had clearly worked its way deep into her psyche. And that was standing in the way of getting her, and her son, the help they needed.

"You can't scrounge your way north and then west," I told her. "Then south again. Washington is a long way."

"We'll make it."

I laid a hard stare on her and, making sure her son wasn't looking, I shook my head—*no you won't.*

"I just need to find enough food," she said. "Then we can get one of the abandoned cars running and..."

There was a fairytale quality to how she was expressing her plans, and it quickly caught up with her. Reality set in and she stared at me, a skim of tears glinting over her gaze. She was afraid.

Damn...

"Okay, you won't come with me," I agreed. "But will you wait here?"

"Why?"

"Because I can be back here with food for you tonight."

She puzzled visibly at my plan. At my offer. For an instant as I conceived it, I did as well. To get home and back in the time I was promising I'd have to hustle my ass on foot, then risk putting my truck on the road to get supplies back here. Then I'd return home, in a truck growling along the silent highway. Anyone within earshot would hear it, and, as I'd just learned, even apparently decent people tended now to respond with, at the minimum, the threat of force.

We were long past the time of handshakes as initial greetings.

"You'd do that?" Sarah asked, truly asked, as if expecting I would up and reveal that it was just some sick joke I was proposing.

"I will."

She glanced down to her son, nuzzled against her, his eyes closed. He was sleeping, the state of rest stealing him fast from the waking world, exhaustion trumping their interaction with a stranger.

"Thank you," Sarah said, managing a smile as a single tear spilled from each eye.

I rose from my crouch and looked behind, to the door that was not that anymore. Wind pushed dust down the street outside. The day was more than half done, sun already taking aim at the western horizon. In a few hours it would be setting. My trip back here would be in the dark.

Nineteen

I sensed something was wrong a hundred yards from my refuge as I was about to cross Weiland Road. Night was rolling over the hills, the glow ahead of me to the west dimming by the minute. But not enough that I couldn't see the collection of empty boxes scattered along the road, cardboard brown, flaps ripped, as if opened with haste. Familiar boxes. Ones that had, until recently, been packed with MREs.

Checking both directions for any sign of life, I jogged to the center of the road and crouched near one of the boxes. On one flap I could plainly see markings that were more than familiar. These marking were mine, done with my own hand while organizing my cache of food soon after settling in. I'd dated and labeled each case. And here one, minus its precious contents, lay in the middle of the road.

I looked across to the vague notch in the forest that was all that remained of the driveway I'd obliterated. Limbs snapped from the dying pines lay haphazardly across the onetime path, several splintered further. As if stepped on.

Forcing myself to move cautiously, I worked my way alongside the hidden driveway, until it lay clear again a distance up from the road. Another box lay there, flaps sealed, the MREs still within. I left it and continued, emerging from the path through the forest to see my refuge in the fading light of day, the barn doors flung open, more boxes of my food cache strewn about.

"Shit..."

My AR at the ready, I approached the barn and peeked past the open door. The shed I'd built within the old structure, crafted to keep half of my food secure from vermin and any encroaching weather, was wrenched open, thin steel walls torn from the metal frame. Whoever had raided my cache hadn't even bothered with the shed's locked door.

I entered the barn and surveyed the loss. The shed was empty. Completely. Fifty percent of what I'd stored was gone. A full ninety percent of my MREs. The only thing left was just what I'd kept in...

...the house.

Damn!

I bolted from the barn and across the dusty courtyard, slipping past my truck and onto the porch, my boots skidding to a stop, almost too fast, my balance precarious for an instant as I grabbed the railing and steadied myself. Where I'd expected to find my front door smashed in, it hung intact on its frame. I unlocked it and moved through the house, less wary than a few moments before. Nothing within was amiss. Everything was how I'd left it. Doors and windows were secure. The remainder of my food supply, split between several closets and a spare bedroom, was untouched. The raiders hadn't bothered with my house.

But why?

I went outside again and headed for the barn, wanting to take a more thorough inventory. But I never made it. Something caught my eye, on the ground just behind where my truck was parked.

Shell casings. A dozen or so. I crouched and picked one up. A .223 caliber. The same as my AR.

I made sure my safety was off and stood, scanning the trees as night began to fill the space between them with shadows. Beyond having a sizable portion of my stores stolen, there'd been gunplay at my refuge. I had no clue as to why.

Until I saw the corner of the barn. Easily missed in my focus on the theft, the pair of holes in the old wood were starkly clear now, about a foot apart, one higher than the other. About head height. The other one lower. Just feet away lay a trio of MRE cases that had been dropped.

It hadn't been just gunplay, I realized. There was a firefight here. A small one, to be certain. Contained. Seemingly initiated when someone shot at those who were raiding my barn. The other boxes scattered down the driveway and in the road beyond gave credence to this. Those who'd come to steal had run off. Had been driven off.

By someone.

I could have spent hours staring into the woods as darkness set, but I'd made a promise. A promise I now had to reconsider. The plentiful store of food I'd known was now halved. Going forward, every bite I took would matter more, because I was that much closer to the state I'd found Sarah and Jeff in.

You can't leave them like that...

No. I couldn't. I knew that. And I wouldn't.

I set about loading my truck with supplies. As night fell fully on the north of the state I drove slowly down the covert driveway I'd maintained and turned onto the road, headlights blazing, Eureka just a few minutes away.

Twenty

I killed my truck's lights and cruised along the street, weaving slowly around abandoned cars. Blocky bits of safety glass, the remnants of someone's windshield, crunched under my tires as I rolled to a stop in front of *Keeping It Reel*, lowering my passenger window and shining a flashlight into the store. It was empty.

There was no assurance that Sarah and Jeff would be exactly where I'd left them. There was also no agreement on where to actually meet them. Both facts left me scanning the street ahead, and behind, for any sign of them. But there was none.

I turned off the engine and stepped from my truck, taking my AR in hand as I walked a few yards ahead of the vehicle and stood in the center of the dark road. Streetlamps that once had blazed when the sun was down loomed cold and black now, no power to feed them, the decorative glass fixtures atop broken on near every pole. I'd not wanted to be shut down by the night and made sure the weapon I brought was topped with my one and only piece of night vision optics. I brought the AR up and looked through the stubby scope atop it, the world beyond revealed in shades of greenish grey, the scant ambient light from stars and the fingernail moon amplified to paint an almost cartoonish picture of my surroundings.

My empty surroundings.

"Sarah!" I called out, keeping my eye to the night scope, slowly sweeping the street ahead and behind as I listened for a reply. Listened for anything.

But there was still nothing. No sign of her or her son.

I crept forward slowly, steadily, weapon up, safety now off. A sense of unease rose, the worry hot and bitter in my gut. Something was wrong.

"Jeff!"

I thought the boy might answer if his mother wouldn't. Or couldn't. I was met, again, with a deep quietness. Even the breeze had settled. Eureka and everything in it felt dead.

crack

The sound was small and close, off to my right. I swung my AR that way and scanned the interior of an old diner through my scope. Booths and a long counter and dangling electrical lines were painted with the colors of a neon forest. The space, where the scent of bacon and eggs and food that was fresh had once filled the air, looked deserted. But it was where the sound had come from. I was sure.

"Sarah," I said, almost hushed now, focused hard on the diner. Watching for movement. Listening.

But not closely enough.

"Put your weapon down," Sarah said, from behind me.

I glanced slowly, cautiously over my shoulder and saw her, on the opposite curb, maybe fifteen feet away, the night's din not enough to hide the lever action pointed at my back for the second time in less than six hours.

"What are you doing, Sarah?"

"Put the weapon down," she repeated. "Right now."

"Okay," I said, and eased my AR down, letting it hang from the sling. "There."

"Show me your hands and turn around."

Again, I followed her instructions, hands held before me, gloved fingers splayed wide.

"Jeff, come on out, honey."

From the diner now behind me, Jeff emerged and walked casually past, tossing a look up at me before joining his mother.

"You did good," Sarah told her son, then she focused on me. "Put your weapons on the ground. All of them."

I unclipped the sling from my AR and placed the rifle on the asphalt at my feet, then took the 1911 from the holster on my hip and did the same.

"Why are you doing this?" I asked her. "I have the food for you. Exactly what I promised. I didn't have to come back here."

"I know," she said, then gestured with the muzzle of the lever action for me to back away from my weapons.

"Then why?" I pressed, taking two steps backward as she and her son took twice that many toward me.

"Are the keys in your truck?"

That single question gave me at least part of the answer I sought.

"You're doing this for my truck? There have to be a dozen cars on this street you could get running. You said that was your plan."

For a moment she said nothing. Just fixed an uncomfortable stare on me.

"Jeff, take his guns and put them in the alley behind the diner."

Her son approached me as instructed and crouched to retrieve my weapons.

"The safeties are off, Jeff," I warned him. "Keep your fingers off the triggers."

"I will," he assured me, then gathered up my rifle and pistol and disappeared back into the deserted eatery.

Sarah took another few steps toward me, the lever action now directed squarely at my gut.

"You're right," she said. "I could have taken another car, but how long would it run? And what would I do if it broke down in the middle of nowhere. There's a lot of nowhere we're going to have to travel through cutting across Canada to get to Washington. It's winter. I can't chance letting my son freeze to death." She nodded toward my truck. "You were prepared for this. More than I was. Your truck has to be in good shape, probably full of gas."

"Diesel," I corrected her.

"I'm sorry."

Jeff returned through the diner and walked toward my truck—now, apparently, *their* truck, and waited.

"Food's in the back," I told Sarah. "There's a good three weeks in there. Plus three five gallon water cans, light sticks, a few other things I thought you might need."

The shame showed plain on her face as I ticked off the things I'd brought her.

"You didn't have to do this."

"Really?" she asked quietly, wanting the exchange to be between just the two of us. "You would have just handed over the keys to your transportation if I needed it?"

"Yes," I said, nodding lightly.

On her face I saw the sense of shame double. She was taking this hard, what she felt she'd been forced to do.

"I hope you make it," I said, and even in the weak light of distant stars I could see her eyes begin to glisten. "I truly hope you get to Bremerton and find your husband. Families should be together."

She didn't move. The lever action seemed to sag in her grip. I probably could have made a move for it. More than likely could have seized it and taken my truck and its contents and left the woman and her son to fend for themselves.

But I didn't.

"Your son's waiting," I said. "Get him out of the cold."

The lever action lowered completely now, muzzle pointed at the dirty roadway. Sarah stood silent, barely holding it.

"Go," I urged her.

"I'm..."

She couldn't manage another apology and simply turned away and climbed into the truck, her son following. Its engine rumbled, the lights came on, and Sarah steered it through a tight one-eighty, putting the left front tire over the curb, and headed off, disappearing down the street and around a corner.

I made my way through the diner and retrieved my weapons. I'd hiked home once already from Eureka. Doing the same in the dark would likely halve the pace I could manage, unless I stuck to the highway.

That wasn't an option. If half of what Sarah had hinted at happening in Whitefish was true, I wanted no chance that some patrol from there might spot me. My refuge had already been raided. If it was some group from down south, affiliated with this Major character, a return visit wasn't out of the question. Neither was an ambush as I returned home. So the woods, thinned and dying, were the way I had to travel. Whatever cover they would provide was more than I could expect on or near the two lanes of asphalt between Eureka and points south.

As I began my trek home, though, I reminded myself that, even without some party waiting to ambush me, there was still at least one someone in the vast, greying woods surrounding my refuge. Someone who'd watched me, and, if indications were what they seemed, used force to, in essence, protect me. The human race was in full retreat, dying off, even killing itself, so it seemed. But in no way could I consider myself alone.

I wanted to believe that was a good thing.

Part Three

Del

Twenty One

It had begun to snow as I reached my house near daybreak, the building layer of white showing no hint of tracks, human or other, prowling around my refuge. A full thirty minutes I'd waited on the hill to the north, watching, searching, trying to pick out any hint of movement, before entering my house and collapsing onto my bed. I knew I had to sleep. But every sound I heard, inside and outside, screamed 'intruder' to me. The wind whipping bare branches against one another set my nerves on edge. The rustle of snow tossed against the windows by the stiffening breeze. In the end, pure exhaustion dragged me down, and I slept the day away, waking as the blizzard darkened with night descending.

The embers I'd left in the hearth sparked a fast fire once I awoke, the fresh logs I fed it catching quickly. The blight had turned the forest to kindling. That was good for the purpose of maintaining warmth. It would be far from welcome should a bolt of lightning strike in the dry season.

I stirred a mix of dried chicken and vegetables into a pot, added some water and a can of broth, and set it on the stove. Next, and maybe more importantly, I plugged the coffee pot in. With the storm blotting the day's sun, and snow skimming my solar panels to further reduce their output, I had to be mindful of my power usage and the drain it would have on my battery array. But coffee was coffee, and as long as my supply lasted, I was going to indulge, especially after the previous day and night I'd endured.

The dinner finished cooking and I ate it from the pot, a half-civilized routine I'd gotten into to save water. There was little point in dirtying a plate, which would then have to be washed, preferably with hot water, something that consumed even more power. The spoon I could lick clean like a ravenous child and then wash thoroughly in the morning when powering up the water heater for a shower. I was trying to be smart about things.

Of course, letting a stranger steal my truck during an act of kindness might count against me in the brains department.

Beep.

The alert sound was light and just audible above the boiling dinner and percolating coffee. I stepped toward the doorway between the kitchen and the front of the house and immediately saw the alarm panel, a single light flashing on the outer perimeter sensors. A thermal one. Something big and warm had encroached upon my property.

Beep.

A second sensor tripped, this one detecting motion. The flashing light on the panel told me it was closer in than the first.

Someone was coming.

I quickly killed the lights inside, not wanting to be silhouetted in the fading day outside. My AR with the tactical scope leaned against the back of a chair facing the hearth. I grabbed it and moved to the front door.

Beep.

Yet another motion sensor was registering a presence, now passing through my inner ring of alert, in a direct line from the previous locations. If I drew a line through them, it would lead right to my house.

I had company.

Weather be damned, I ignored the cold and stepped onto my porch, a steady dump of snow drifting down from above. I advanced to the edge of the porch where it turned to wrap around the south side and crouched, leaning my AR and a portion of my upper body around the corner to scan the near whiteout beyond. Full darkness had not yet settled, and the veil of snow took on a thick, opaque quality, like drizzling flakes of fog floating in the half light. It obscured almost everything beyond a few yards. I could just make out the edge of the dead woods.

And the man emerging from the trees.

"Hello!" he said.

I zeroed in on him through the scope, bright reticle on his chest. The slim barrel of a rifle pointed upward from his back, and his hands were empty, one raised in greeting.

"Who are you?" I challenged the man.

"My name is Del Drake," he answered. "I'm the one who put a couple holes in your barn."

This was my visitor. My watcher. And, it seemed, my protector.

"All right if I come on over?"

I eased my eye from the scope and looked to the vague shape with my naked eye. It seemed some moment of truth was at hand. I'd been waylaid and robbed by strangers twice in the previous days. Now, here was another unknown presenting himself. Wanting to enter my refuge. Neil might advise me to tell the armed enigma to do a one-eighty and make his way back to wherever he'd come from, and my friend might be right.

Might be.

Could I risk more contact with an outsider? Or was it just as much a risk to turn this outsider, who had done what he could to salvage a good portion of my food from being appropriated by the raiding party?

The truth be told, the man standing in the snow might be the closest thing to a friend I had at the moment.

"Yeah," I said, standing and lowering my AR. "Come on."

Del tramped the dozen yards or so to my porch and found shelter from the storm, tossing back the hood of his parka and smiling at me through a trimmed but full beard. He offered the hand he had waved with, and the other I now saw was not empty, but cradled a medium-size clear jar, a mass of bright orange something within.

"An apology for drilling those shots into your barn," Del said as he handed the jar to me. "Peaches I canned before...before everything went to shit."

I eyed the jar and its clearly delicious contents. It had been weeks since anything truly fresh had slipped past my lips, and I was already imagining the glorious taste to be had.

"No apology necessary," I told Del. "You saved me from starving. If they'd gotten in my house..."

"Well," he began, "I wasn't going to let that happen."

Again he smiled, sincere and warm. I felt instantly at ease with the man.

"You up for some bad coffee?" I asked him.

"Exactly what I make myself," he said, laughing a bit.

"Come on in."

* * *

Del leaned his rifle against the wall and eased himself into one of the chairs facing the hearth, smiling against some discomfort as he settled into the cushions. I took the other chair and eyed him.

"You okay?"

He shrugged off the concern with a nod and sipped at the mug of coffee I'd poured him.

"Cup of Joe and someone to talk to," he said, smiling. "What more could a man ask for. Especially these days?"

He had a point. But he was also lying. There was something wrong. The pain he'd tried to mask was too obvious. Too familiar. I'd seen the same in Neil's father during a quick trip I'd taken to see my old friend not quite a year ago. It was right after the man had been diagnosed with the big C, and it was already bad for him. He, too, smiled through the discomfort. Gritted his teeth behind tight lips, not wanting to be a bother. So I knew.

After a moment, maybe seizing upon the hint of doubt in my gaze, Del realized I wasn't being fooled.

"In the bones," Del said. "Found out just before everything went to hell."

"I'm sorry."

"I tell you what," he said, sipping from the mug before continuing, "some oncologist somewhere is going to lose out on a boatload of cash from Medicare."

He laughed. A true laugh. Some ability to make light of his mortality flavoring the gesture.

"I've had sixty-seven years, so far." He wrapped the side table with his knuckles. "If I make it to sixty-eight, that's just gravy. Life's been good." Then his mood darkened, almost instantly. He stared at the fire crackling in the hearth. "Life's different now, though. A year doesn't mean the same thing. Hanging on another three-sixty-five is a lifetime, considering so many are dead and gone."

I leaned forward, cupping my coffee in both hands. We talked for the next twenty minutes about our lives. Where we'd been and how we'd gotten here. Del had moved to his remote hideaway forty years ago, and worked logging crews in both Montana and Idaho for the better part of the last thirty years, until retiring a few years back. He'd been married once, for a short while, but the isolation, which he favored, wore on her, and on their union. It was odd—here was a man nearly twice my age, who lived a mile away over a stubby mountain, and, without ever laying eyes on him before this, I felt I knew him, I understood him, better than most people I'd called friends for twenty years.

All but Neil.

"How'd you figure it out?"

"Figure what out?" I asked, and Del smiled, which was enough to set me on the right path. "Yeah, this."

"Tell you how I knew," Del began. "Toilet paper."

I chuckled.

"Go ahead and laugh, but a readily available supply of toilet paper is the indicator of a stable civilization. When I saw folks hoarding that on a trip to town before I holed up, I knew. People were worried about this."

People...

One species of many on this rock spinning through space. We used to count our number in billions. And now...

"How many do you think are left?"

Del thought for a moment. Not like someone performing any calculation derived from points of accuracy. But like a man peering into some nightmare made real, its consequences plain to know.

"Most everyone's met their maker by now," he said solemnly. "Good and bad, old and young. Starvation favors the last man with crumbs, and the crumbs are nearly gone." His gaze shifted toward me. "You and me, we've got some crumbs. That's why we're still here. But you've gotta learn from your mistakes."

"What mistakes?"

He tipped his head toward the fire, its flames licking furiously upward, tossing a welcome warmth into the room.

"That's how they found you," Del said. "In this wasteland you can smell smoke ten miles away. And what you're putting out that chimney is easy to spot against the daytime sky. All they did was follow their noses, and then use their eyes."

I looked to the fire. It was sometimes my method of cooking, to conserve what propane remained. My sole source of warmth.

"Harder to see smoke on most nights, so a smaller fire is usually okay after dark," he said. "Smell will still carry."

"Wonderful," I said. "I put a damn target on myself and didn't even realize it."

"Well, they were looking."

I sat back again and sipped at my coffee.

"Pretty sure I saw 'em before," Del began. "Coming up from Kalispell, I thought. I was doing a little multi-day recon down south past Whitefish when I spotted them. Whole gypsy train of people. Mostly men, all armed. They had three vehicles pulling trailers. Scavenging then, I suppose, just like they were when they hit you."

"When was this?"

"A few weeks back. Around the time we got our first snow."

First snow...

"I heard some shooting around then," I told him. "Helluva firefight south of here."

"I heard that, too."

"Was that them?"

His brow shrugged. "I split off from watching them just outside Kalispell to head back this way. No point in taking a chance on them seeing me."

"Why?"

"On the roof of one of their trucks they'd mounted a machine gun," Del said. "Probably stole it off a wrecked Guard vehicle. There's enough of them and their weaponry laying around to..."

He seemed to not want to say what had to come next.

"...equip a small army?"

He nodded and I told him about what Sarah had shared. About someone calling himself the Major exerting authority in Whitefish. And maybe beyond that, if his people were the ones who'd raided my refuge.

"Could just be rumors," Del suggested.

"She seemed pretty freaked by this guy."

"I haven't ventured into Whitefish, so can't say one way or another," Del said. "So, you took this woman and her son some food, did you?"

I nodded. Then I told him about my truck, which was *her* truck now.

"Was wondering where that disappeared to," Del said, some slight glint in his eyes. A visual grin. "Heard you leave in it. Didn't hear it come back."

"Ears of a cougar," I commented.

"That's how I knew you were being hit. I heard trucks rumbling up the road and then spotted them from the hill between our properties. You didn't appear to be home, and I suspected that they were not invited, so I drilled a couple rounds close enough to scatter them. If I'd gotten to the hill sooner they might not have gotten away with any of your supplies." He held a palm out toward the roaring fire, its blasting warmth a fading luxury. "One of them took some shots back. Just wild blasts. He had a rifle like yours."

My AR. Resting on the table behind us. Del's choice of long gun was far more basic. A scoped bolt action Remington 700 in .308. Damn fine weapon, equally capable caliber, but nowhere near as able as my semi-auto to lay down fire fast on multiple targets.

"Old school," I observed, gesturing to the Remington, and Del nodded.

"Distance is your friend," Del said. "It's best to avoid threats. If you can't, it's best to deal with them before they get close."

Wise words. They seemed to come naturally to Del Drake. That was an appraisal based on all of the hour I'd known him, but I believed it to be true. I believed him to be true.

"I'm glad you stopped them before they cleaned me out," I said, smiling. Thinking. Remembering. The sensation I'd had after erasing my driveway's connection to the road. That feeling that someone was in the woods.

Watching. "You've been keeping an eye on me, haven't you?"

"I wouldn't call it that," Del said, smiling, an almost impish grin ducking behind the mug as he drank.

"What then?" I smirked a bit. "Just a recon of the neighbor?"

"There's an old saying: good fences make good neighbors." Del let that hang for a moment. "Bullshit. Good neighbors make good neighbors. I needed to know that you were that."

He was smart. And honest. Those were two qualities I'd learned were increasingly uncommon in the world. Or the world that was. Now the ratio had been skewed, the pools of the right-minded and the foolhardy oversampled. It seemed to me that, among survivors, there would be a fair amount of smart ones to be found.

If only that also meant they weren't dangerous.

"You fixed my propane regulator," I said, the realization coming quietly, born of the obvious.

"Didn't know if your place was going to sit vacant," Del said. "Until you showed, I thought you'd end up like most folks. I figured if that was the case, your propane shouldn't just bleed out."

"Hell, I'd want you to have it," I told him. "If I kick tomorrow, feel free to whatever I've got. No sense in it going to waste."

"Likewise," Del said, and that was it, an agreement no different than a last will and testament. Made by two men without a lawyer so much as breathing within miles. No paper. No handshake, even. Just our words, and, more importantly, our understanding of what we both faced.

The fire began to quiet, log splitting atop the pile, a flourish of embers swirling up the chimney. I could already feel the night's coming chill working to tame the heat.

"I've got to admit," I said, "I'm going to miss a fire at night."

"Iron stove in your bedroom?"

"Yeah." It was an ancient thing, made when objects were art, crafted by someone with an eye for scrollwork, ribbons of pounded and shaped metal brazed to the door and around the rim to contain any pot one might place upon it to be warmed. The most I'd done on it was heat a kettle of water for tea when I was sick one day, preferring to stay in bed and nurse the nasty bug away with copious amounts of chamomile. "I'm going to need a pile of blankets to replace what it puts out."

"I wouldn't say that."

I looked to Del. He raised a hand a bit and extended his index finger.

"Just one will do."

"I'm not following you."

Del smiled and pushed himself up from the chair.

"Feel like taking a walk?" he asked.

I looked through the window. The blizzard had waned. Just the fluff of a wintry sky drifting down now. Still, Del could spot the doubt in my gaze.

"The walk will warm you up for the night," he said.

"Okay."

I had no idea what Del Drake wanted to show me, but after what he'd already done for me, indulging him with a trudge through a mile of ankle deep snow was the least I could do.

Twenty Two

Forty five minutes it took us to reach Del's house, following a trail worn thinly through the dying woods, bare branches above shielding enough of the forest floor from the storm just ended to allow the path to be made out. He'd been careful to not leave obvious tracks, just nonspecific tells of the way to go. A twisted sapling. A rock on its end. But even in the dark, moving only by the meager glow of our headlamps, Del never lost the trail. These woods were his woods. He was intimate with them. In them every day for four decades.

He likely knew them better than any person.

He took me straight through his modest house, its walls roughhewn lumber, rustic and warm, like someone had slapped a roof on the forest, to the only bedroom in the back.

"There you go," he said, gesturing at his old bed, a thin layer of comforter atop it.

Then I saw the wire. It snaked from beneath the comforter to an electrical inverter in the corner, deep cycle battery wired to it. A pair of cables were tacked to the wall and disappeared through a precisely cut hole in the timber ceiling.

"Electric blanket?"

Del nodded.

"I have it set on a timer," he explained as I went to the bed and examined the setup he'd constructed. "It runs fifteen minutes every hour through the night. Keeps me toasty. The battery's good for a full night, then charges the next day. I don't have it wired into the rest of the circuits. That way if the timer craps out and it turns on, it will only drain this battery."

"You hooked to solar?"

"That and a hydro impeller," Del explained, revealing that at least part of his energy needs were being met by a pint-size version of hoover dam. "I have it set in the creek out back. Even when it freezes there's enough flow under the ice to keep a few lights on and keep me warm."

"Unbelievable," I commented. "This is stupid simple, which means I should have thought of it."

"You could rig one up at your place to keep the smoke signature down. I have an extra timer thingamajig you could wire in. All you'd need is the electric blanket."

That I didn't have. And I wasn't sure where to get one.

"I could try scavenging a store, I guess."

Del shook his head, not keen on that idea.

"You'd be better off trying some abandoned houses," he suggested. "Away from any sizeable population. Just in case that Major fella isn't a rumor."

It was a good idea. Glancing at the method of staying warm he'd crafted, I could see that Del Drake was brimming with them.

"Wanna see something else?"

"Sure," I said.

Del led me down a short hallway, to a door that, if the implied layout of his house was correct, should be a second bedroom. It was and it wasn't.

"Holy...." I exclaimed in a slightly truncated fashion as he opened the door.

"My favorite place in the whole damn universe," he said.

I stepped past Del and marveled at the array of amateur radio equipment that filled the room he'd led me to, its modernity so conflicted with the basic, Spartan existence he'd constructed that it was almost jarring.

"Unbelievable."

Every display, every light, every dial was dark, but it took little effort to imagine the space as something close to mission control at NASA.

Del stepped to a breaker box on the wall and threw a switch, then powered up the radios and their corresponding devices so that I didn't have to imagine anymore.

"This beats the radio at my construction yard," I told him.

"About all she's good for right now is looking at."

I puzzled visibly at Del's statement, and he lowered himself into the chair at the center of the station and turned the volume dial up. All that came through was the insidiously familiar.

"Red... Red... Red..."

He turned the volume down and switched the array of electronics off.

"At least when that stops you might be able to contact someone," I suggested, and to that Del half shrugged.

"If it stops."

"It can't go on forever."

"Doesn't have to," he said, smiling. "Just has to outlast you, and me, and anyone else who was smart enough or tough enough to hang on. You see, it's really us who can't go on forever."

He had a point. A cold, brutally blunt point. We were an endangered species.

"Besides, reaching out with my rig is no different than you sending a plume of smoke up from your chimney. That just announces that someone's here."

"So, you won't use it if the Red Signal stops?"

He looked past me, to a closet in the corner, the door partly open, stacked spools of thick black wire within.

"If I do decide to, I'll reposition the antenna off over the hill to the south," Del explained. "I've got about two thousand feet of coax cable and a half dozen signal boosters. Anyone tracking the signal would zero in on that, not where we're standing."

"Still pretty damn close," I said, and Del nodded.

"Too close, probably. It might be necessary to just remain a voyeur of the airwaves," he said. "Never seen, never heard, but always listening."

That would require someone to listen to, an increasingly doubtful certainty.

We chatted for a few minutes, then I thanked Del. For defending my refuge, the peaches, his idea on how to stay warm without giving my location away. In a way, though, I was expressing my gratitude for his presence. For the first time since the Red Signal, I could truly say that I did not feel one hundred percent alone. There was another person like me. To talk to. To help. To seek help from.

I needed to act on the suggestion he'd given me. An electric blanket was top of the list of needs now. Traveling to Whitefish was out of the question, and there was no guarantee in any case that what I was seeking would exist there in any of the stores that had certainly been looted. Eureka, too, would likely be a fool's errand. As Del said, a house was the most likely place to find what I sought. North of my refuge, some miles before Eureka, there was a place I could try. That I would try. A hopefully simple errand that would take half a day at most.

I had no idea someone would die because of it.

Twenty Three

The weather was doable as I set out in the morning, but the air had that feel to it, cold on top of cold that hinted at another storm moving it. All I could do was hope that it would hold off until I made it back home.

I reached the railroad tracks where they curved west from the highway, then followed their gentle arc north. Every few hundred yards I'd stop and survey the way ahead through my binoculars, especially when the landscape opened to fields, dead grey skimmed with winter white. Where once I might have seen lines of tracks crossing the snowy expanse, or seen hawks circling above, there existed now just pristine frozen fields. Unmarked. The hollow flatness yet another sign of death.

The plants had died. Then the animals that ate the plants. Then the animals that ate those animals. Along with humans who ranched them and cut them into steaks and chops. Every living thing, it seemed, was paying the price. The blight ruled.

Somewhere, I imagined, there was still animal life. A hearty squirrel subsisting on what he'd stored. A grizzly, maybe, who'd made it to their winter den before wasting away. Some birds, I suspected, would hang on, at least those that could pluck fish from the lakes. Until, of course, whatever plant-borne nutrients the fish needed were ravaged, if they hadn't been already.

But the scarcity of life was welcome, at least to me. At least during the time of my quick trek northward. I did not want to run across anyone. Anyone at all. Odd as that might seem, in a world where contact and companionship was the holy grail of existence, my experience, other than Del, had been marked by danger and deceit. By conflict. By threat. To do this, alone, and encounter no one, be they benign or otherwise, was my plan.

Fortine, Montana. That's where the tracks led me before they stitched on toward Eureka. It could hardly be branded a town. Fifty or sixty people had called it home. I'd expected it would be far less jarring a sight than what I'd encountered on my trip to Eureka.

I was wrong.

Fortine sat still and ravaged. Peering down what passed for the main drag through town, with the railroad tracks behind, I took stock of the devastation. Most of the hamlet's few buildings were blackened by fire. Windows shattered in those that still stood. Furniture stripped from business and home alike and strewn about yard and street. Abandoned cars dotted the street, some parked nonchalantly, and others nosed over gutters, or plowed into trees, windshields riddled with bullets.

Then there were the bodies. None parted and stripped for cooking by cannibals as I'd seen on my visit some miles to the north. These lay in gutters, or sat slumped behind steering wheels, bloated and decaying, what birds remained having picked skin and flesh from several.

Directly across the street from me, a near skeletal sculpture of mother and child leaned against a wall near the shattered entrance of the Post Office, holding each other, the both of them little more than bone and skin beneath layers of clothing. The blight had taken them, in its own way, its own time. Starvation. An agonized churning in their stomach. That's how they'd gone. Their final days, hours, and minutes had been hell.

I stepped around the corner and looked away from the mother and child. Beings that could have been Sarah and her son, Jeff, had they not escaped from Whitefish, and then Eureka. It might still be the fate they found, but I hoped not. Looking ahead I scanned for movement and listened for sound. I saw only the remnants of the once charming burg. Heard only the breeze working on the torn flaps of an awning dangling from its frame outside a scorched structure.

Beyond the obvious devastation I saw two houses, unburnt, their doors open. Curtains whipped past the broken glass held jagged in the window frames. I approached, my AR at the ready, snow crackling beneath my boots, no stealth in my movement. No cover for it, either. Anyone watching, or listening, should they have any sort of serviceable firearm, would be able to end me. It was a risk, I knew. But there was no other way to the houses.

I reached the first one and waited, ears tuned beyond the wind to any sound that might be manmade. There was none. The house was newer, likely built as a getaway not unlike the one I'd planned at my property. Its front steps groaned ever so slightly as I mounted them and stood staring into the dark interior, flickers of light trickling in through shattered panes revealing the shadowed shell of a home.

Broken bits of glass grated between my boots and the tiled entry as I stepped inside. The place had been ransacked, but not looted. Items that might have been taken otherwise were toppled, but still on premises. A television. DVD player. Chairs and couches.

But every cabinet, and the silent refrigerator, was open, any semblance of edibles within gone. Calories had surpassed currency as the thieves' target of choice in this new world.

I waded through the house, to the bedrooms at the rear, sprawling deck beyond the largest, a gorgeous master suite. Drawers of a toppled bureau had been jerked free in here and tossed about, contents scattered. Including...

"You've gotta be kidding," I said aloud upon seeing the electric blanket, still mostly folded, its cord trailing away and dangling over the edge of an upturned drawer.

The first house I'd searched, with hardly any effort put into the act other than a moderate hike, and there it was. Luck, divine providence, whatever it was, I was thankful for the break I'd been dealt. It could just as easily been a day wasted, pawing through residence after residence.

I gathered the item up and, without thinking, brought the cord to an outlet to test it before the folly of that action set in. Power had likely stayed on for some time after the Red Signal. But those running and maintaining the generating plants, and the lines that brought electricity to cities and towns and outlying settlements like Fortine, were no different than the skeletal woman down the road. Some might have stayed at their jobs for a week, maybe two, as starvation became not something to worry about, but a reality to face. Beyond that, they would have weakened. They would have sought sustenance. Spent their waning hours with whatever family they still had. The power they once worked to supply would have disappeared, bit by bit, area by area, as components failed, or safety systems kicked in. Sabotage might have taken some grids down. But everywhere that did not have its own supply of energy would be dark, with outlets like the one I was looking at cold and useless.

I tucked the electric blanket into the small backpack I brought with me and headed out of the bedroom. At the door I stopped and looked to the light switch. It was in the off position. With a bit of nostalgia for the recent past I flipped it upward, but the fixture at the center of the room stayed dark.

"Home," I said to the emptiness, ready to make my way south.

The man with the hatchet standing in the living room as I came down the hallway seemed ready to prevent that.

"Give me your food."

What he said didn't surprise me. It differed little from what Sarah had insisted from me. She, though, said it past the barrel of a gun. This man, wasted to angular bones beneath nearly translucent skin, was giving me an order with a dull, rusted hand-axe trembling in his weak grip.

"I don't have any food," I told the man, right thumb flipping the safety on my AR to fire.

"You...look at you...you have to have food!"

He raised the hatchet, the fifteen feet separating us uncomfortably close, even with his strength lacking and the implement less than ideal. It could do damage. Damage I didn't want to deal with. Not if I could prevent it.

"Back away," I said, raising the AR and taking aim at him. "Now!"

My forcefulness, I hoped, would compel him to retreat. Or, at least, reconsider any further advance. Long enough that I could talk him down from the precipice he'd been forced to.

He was beyond dialogue, however.

"Your food!" he shouted, and drew the axe back as he took a step toward me. Then another.

I fired before he could take a third. Three shots. All hitting their mark at this distance, drilling a triangular pattern of holes in his dirty sweatshirt. He stutter-stepped to the side, still holding the hatchet high, its weight seeming to drag his balance to the left until he toppled over the back of a chair and rolled to the floor, face gaping at the ceiling as bubbles of blood burst from his mouth.

"Dammit," I said, resisting the urge to rush forward and help the man. He'd been willing to attack me, I had to remind myself. To kill me, almost certainly. He was either mad with hunger, or simply mad, driven to that state of mental collapse by what had befallen all that surrounded him. By things he'd seen, or experienced.

And despite whatever sympathy I felt for his plight, the hatchet still rested in his hand, fingers curled around the old handle, flexing open and closed, gripping and releasing, gripping and releasing. His gaze, though, was not directed toward me. Instead it drifted lazily at the ceiling, disconnected, as if he was trying to seize the vision of something beyond it. Some place. Or someone.

"I'll get the food," the man said, his voice softening toward a whisper. "I'll get it, sweetie."

My aim shifted off of the man. His hand opened, fingers unfurling from around the hatchet's handle.

"We'll have all the..."

He coughed, a shallow belch of air and bloody mist rising from his mouth.

"All the..."

Was this just a conversation the man was having with a memory? With the ghost of a loved one already gone? It had to be. It had to.

"Sweetie..."

That was his last word. The punctuation of his life. Then his last breath hissed almost silently out, and he was gone.

I didn't move for several minutes. The sight of him, of the man I'd just killed, held me rapt. He lay there, anonymous. I knew nothing of him but his desperation. Did he live in Fortine? Near here? Was this his home? Or was he a wanderer, searching for food? Just a lost soul stumbling toward the inevitable.

Finally, I looked away, and moved past him, to the front door and onto the porch. I stood there and looked to the town in the near distance, roofs heavy with snow. The wind picked up, whistling through the naked trees as I began to weep.

Twenty Four

I stared at the floor in Del's living room as he tipped the whiskey bottle again, adding a splash to the mug in my hand.

"More," he said. "Go on."

Already I'd had the equivalent of three shots. But the numbness I felt had nothing to do with the alcohol. I brought the drink to my lips and drained what he'd poured me in one fast swallow.

Del sat in a chair across the coffee table from where I sat on the couch. He screwed a cap on the bottle and put it on the table between us.

"You think you had another choice?" Del asked.

I shook my head. I knew what I'd done in Fortine was necessary. But I was shaken by the reality of it. By the *necessity* of having to kill a man.

"You know you didn't," my friend reminded me.

"I know," I said, my hand clenching around the cup. Bearing down. An anger filling me. "I just hate that the world has come to this. And that I have to be part of it."

I'd come straight to Del's, bypassing my refuge. It was late afternoon and cottony flurries had begun to sprinkle from the sky. Beyond the window, in the wintry light, the downy flakes seemed to float like feathers.

"Yeah, you're part of it," Del said. "*Still* part of it. If that guy had taken you out, what would he have gotten? Anything? You didn't have food. From how you described him he sounds like he was at death's door already."

"Are you suggesting I did him a favor?"

"No," Del said, shaking his head. "You did yourself a favor. You survived. That's what everything is about, isn't it?"

You've gotta hang on, Fletch. Okay? You have to. Stay alive.

Neil's words, almost his final ones to me, surfaced like some talisman.

Stay alive. Stay alive. Stay alive.

"Yeah," I told Del. Maybe not fully accepting it yet, but agreeing.

He took the bottle and was about to pour me yet another when I waved him off.

"Have I mentioned that I don't drink?"

"Neither do I," Del said. "Why do you think the bottle was full?"

I laughed lightly. It felt good to do so. Some small bit of relief was washing over me. Not absolution for what I'd done, but a modicum of willingness to believe that I was in the right.

If there could be anything resembling 'right' in what had transpired in Fortine.

"You want to hear something odd?"

A distraction. I would welcome it, in any form, though I immediately wondered if Del was simply trying to help shift my thoughts from the day's events. I nodded and sat back to listen.

"I took a little walk myself today while you were gone," he said. "A couple miles west to an old friend's cabin. Name's Eddie Martin. I'd been curious about him since all this started. He was a part timer up here, weekends and summers. The rest of the time he spent in Kalispell."

"Retired?"

"From the railroad. I didn't expect to find him there, and he wasn't. But something was."

I leaned forward now, sensing some gravity to Del's tone.

"The place was booby trapped."

"What?"

"Yeah," Del said. "Trip wire at the back, at the base of the stoop below the door. And some sort of pressure deal inside the front door. I decided to look through the windows after I spotted what was waiting out back."

"What was it wired to?"

"The inside one, I never tried to get close. The one out back was hooked to four sticks of trinitrotoluene under the stoop."

"TNT?"

"Blasting caps with one second fuses on each," he said.

"Shit."

"Indeed," Del said, reaching for a small satchel next to the couch. He passed it to me. "Have a look."

I looked at the bag, zipped shut, incredulous.

"You're kidding."

"Had to mess with the stuff when I worked in logging back in the day," he explained.

I unzipped the satchel and parted the opening, looking in to see four sticks of TNT, the rusty paper wrapping each blotched by the weather.

"It had been there a while," Del said. "A few weeks at least."

"But after all this started?"

He nodded. I zipped the satchel back up and set it gingerly on the floor.

"Who set the trap?"

Del thought for a moment, no more clarity coming from the question I posed than the same he'd mulled most of the day.

"Eddie, maybe," Del suggested, his heart clearly not in that scenario. "But I can't come up with a reason why."

"To stop someone from getting in?"

"And destroy the place in the process?" Del asked, shaking his head. "That's pretty damn extreme."

Del was right. What could the man expect to achieve through destroying his own property to protect it? So maybe...

"How close is Eddie's place to the road?" I asked. "I mean, is it more accessible than either of our properties?"

"Twenty feet off the road," Del answered. "You can see it driving by. Plus he's got this big mailbox he carved to look like a grizzly head with its mouth open."

I looked away for a moment, convinced that my supposition was likely fact.

"What?" Del asked, seeing the mental gears churning behind my eyes.

"Remember the woman, Sarah?"

"Yeah."

"She told me that this Major guy wasn't letting anyone leave Whitefish. He was telling them that if they tried to go anywhere, even to a cabin near town, they'd be killed."

It was registering with Del. He straightened in his chair, the pain evident in his face, along with something else.

Fury. Cold, quiet, measured hate.

"He's penning them up," Del said. "And if the warnings aren't enough, he booby-traps a few places where people might hide from him. Boom. What a message that would send."

If this was true, if I was actually right, there was something that, especially now, didn't make sense.

"What about me?" I asked Del.

"What about you?"

"The raiders, the ones who hit my place, if they were his..."

"Why haven't they come back?" Del asked for me.

"They know someone is there. Someone with food."

"The fact that they were chased off by an old man with a bolt action rifle might inform their decision to steer clear."

"They had no idea who you were," I reminded him. "They knew nothing about you."

"They knew someone on this mountain was prepared to shoot back."

He had a point. In the classic sense, the Major, and those allied with him, were bullies. When faced with a victim who fought back, bullies tended to reconsider their victim. Or their approach.

"So I get a pass?"

"For the moment," Del said. "But once he feels secure, once he's built up his forces from the locals, they'll be back."

"Wonderful," I said, looking to the bottle on the coffee table. "I think I might start not drinking again."

I held the mug out and Del poured me a splash of courage.

"I think maybe we need to lay eyes on just what's happening down in Whitefish," Del said. "Before it comes our way."

I took a long drink and nodded.

Twenty Five

The train tracks that had led me out of Whitefish on the day the Red Signal appeared now led Del and I back toward the town. A mile from it, near two in the afternoon, we came upon the first horror that seemed to validate the fear Sarah had expressed.

"Christ," Del said softly.

Both of us saw it at the same time as we emerged from the trees on the west side of Whitefish Lake, facing a house just inland from Beaver Bay. A galvanized fencepost had been driven into the earth in front of the residence, its upper end hidden somewhere within the man who'd been impaled upon it, his body inverted, pole disappearing into his mouth as if he'd swallowed it. His decaying hands were tied behind his back, feet similarly bound together, the dead holes where his eyes had once been seeming to stare at the sign affixed to the bottom of the post. One word scrawled upon the square placard.

HOARDER

"The new crucifixion," Del commented.

"Sarah said everyone was supposed to turn in their food," I recounted.

"He, apparently, did not."

Cold had helped preserve the corpse somewhat, but it was apparent from the gush of frozen blood spilled down the pole and over the sign that the man had been dealt his fate while alive.

"They watched," I said.

"My guess is they made others watch, too," Del added.

I had to believe that he was right. What we were seeing was as much message as punishment.

"Major James Layton appears to be one piece of work," Del said.

There was every possibility our presence would not be appreciated, particularly being that we were armed and unwilling to follow orders that had been blasted out over the airwaves. Turning back might be the prudent thing to do.

We did not. Both Del and I, as neighbors and friends, needed to know as much as we could about Whitefish. In no small way we were spies on a mission of our own making. And, like intelligence agents in both fact and fiction, were we to be discovered, our lifespan would be measured in minutes, not years.

Another hour it took us, moving from cover to cover, before we reached the western edge of town, beyond the golf course, where houses were spread over large lots of land. The whole of the land before us, dotted with snowy roofs and dead trees stabbing skyward from drifts, gave the appearance of some abandoned alien settlement.

Yet, clearly, what we saw on the road across a barren field proved it had not been rendered lifeless.

Two men, rifles slung on their shoulders, stood in front of a newer pickup, machinegun mounted to a metal framework rising from the bed. They talked, and across the distance we could both hear them occasionally laugh.

Del took his own pair of binoculars out and surveyed the scene, glassing the men, and the road both east and west of them.

"Movement to the east," he said. "Nothing to the west."

"They're sentries," I suggested. "Controlling access."

"We'll find the same on the other roads in and out," Del said, putting his binoculars away. "This way is a no go."

"Let's backtrack, come in from the north through the rail yards."

Del didn't seem entirely enthused by that approach.

"We'll have to chance the rail bridge or the ice to get across the river," he said.

"Ice, I'd say. It'll hold."

"I'm sure it will," Del agreed. "But if we need to get the hell out fast, there'll be a river between us and our way home. Unless you want to take a helluva long walk around the east side of the lake."

It was a risk, to be sure. But we'd come to get information, and we couldn't accomplish that without getting closer. Much closer. Through the rail yards was the best avenue to making that happen. And the safest, in my opinion.

"It's worth the risk," I told Del.

"Okay," he said, without hesitation, trusting in my appraisal.

We followed the path I'd proposed, skirting the sparse number of dwellings on the west side of town, each and every one we passed seeming left to the elements. Windows smashed. Doors wrenched from their hinges.

"Looks like they don't want folks even this far out," Del observed.

"Concentrating the population to control them," I said, echoes of a history almost forgotten rising. "Like a ghetto."

Near the golf course we chanced entering a house, to check its interior, no obvious traps set to deter squatters, though the destruction of its barrier to weather made it all but uninhabitable. What we found inside painted still more of a picture of what had happened. Cabinets were cleaned out. Refrigerator empty. A basement dry room, where the resident had once obviously kept preserved goods and home crafted beers, was empty, the machinery to process the foods gone as well, leaving dusty footprints of where they'd been.

"Turn in your food, right?"

"If they had anything left," I said, mostly agreeing with Del's rhetorical recollection. Most people would have exhausted the food kept in their house within a week. Some, maybe the people in this house, were keepers of preserved foods. Not survivalists, but just individuals who chose to be prepared.

We left the house and continued, crossing the frozen mouth of the river just upstream from the rail bridge spanning it. Shallow water bubbled beneath a few inches of ice, the footing solid as we hurried to the far side and scampered up the embankment. To our left, Whitefish Lake lay still and flat, iced over, a carpet of snow thick atop that. Ahead, the open expanse of the rail yard stretched for hundreds of yards, the space broken by maintenance sheds, trailer offices, and a mix of train cars and one locomotive scattered about the spur lines feeding the main track. Using the structures and cars as cover, Del and I leapfrogged to cross the yard, one moving and then the other, until we had reached the Baker Avenue Bridge. We passed beneath it and found cover behind the museum at the north end of Depot Park.

"There," Del said, pointing around the corner of the trash dumpster.

I tracked his direction and saw a few people down the street, congregating in front of the middle school. None appeared to be armed. Two looked to be women, the other a man much older. He leaned on the women, and their arms curled behind his back, supporting him.

"You notice anything else?" I asked Del.

"You mean how clean it is?"

"Not a wreck on the streets," I said. "Every window I see is unbroken or boarded over."

"We're inside their zone. They don't have to discourage people from being here."

Del was right in his analysis. We'd easily penetrated their perimeter, which, when one considered the facts, was unsurprising. Most of the citizenry was dead and gone. The force that the Major would have arrived with, and built from any willing residents, would hardly be sufficient to seal the town fully. There were too many ways in and out. Fear and intimidation, with maybe a promise of order and food, was enough to keep most every survivor in place. This we knew.

What we didn't know was what their reaction to intruders would be.

"Patrol," Del said, ducking fully behind the dumpster.

I heard the rumble before seeing the two large pickup trucks rumble over the bridge to our right, arriving from the northern part of the town. Each had a machine gun mounted similarly to the vehicle we'd seen at the roadblock. What was different here were the two armed men in the back of each truck, one on the machine gun and the other next to him with an assault rifle at the ready.

"They've been scrounging weapons the Guard left behind," Del said.

From the look of their armament, and what Del described seeing on a scouting trip before we'd met, he was dead on. It made me wonder, with such a display, if they'd tried to disarm the surviving population, maybe taking a cue from FEMA, as indicated on the notice Marco had shown me. No weapons allowed in the camps, centers, whatever they were calling them down in Arizona. If such places existed at all. Or existed anymore. They would have been overrun with refugees, I knew. People just like Marco, desperate for food, and medical care. And stability.

Is that all Major Layton had had to do? Dangle stability in front of the desperate population of a small town, a good portion of which was well armed in their everyday existence? Some had resisted, as Sarah had implied. The firefight I'd watched from a distance now seemed all but certain to have involved the Major's men and noncompliant townspeople.

And it was clear who had won that skirmish.

The patrol worked its way off the bridge and drove through the snowy streets, nearing the trio of people gathered near the middle school. The two vehicles pulled up and stopped, five armed men exiting the vehicles and approaching the people. One man remained on his truck's machine gun, covering not the interaction beginning, but their flanks and rear.

"They don't feel fully secure," I commented as I watched the machine gunner swivel his weapon slowly, searching for threats.

"Compliance hasn't been total," Del said.

The next thing to inform our opinion of the force that had taken over Whitefish was not anything we saw. It was what we heard.

A blood curdling scream rolled up the street from the two women as the older man was pulled from their embrace and dragged toward the lead vehicle. One of the women tried to push past the armed men and she was knocked to the ground, courtesy of a rifle but strike to her back. The other woman dropped to the ground and shielded her companion with her body. The armed men, satisfied that they'd stopped any resistance, returned to their vehicles, the older man heaved roughly into the first truck, only a single man required to keep him subdued as the patrol drove away.

"What the hell was that?"

Del didn't have an immediate answer to my question.

"That guy didn't look like he could muster much trouble for anyone to be concerned with," he observed.

The trucks pulled away and disappeared down the street, the women still huddled on the snowy sidewalk, one hurt and the other sobbing over her.

"They might have some answers for us," Del said.

He was right. But to seek those answers we'd have to expose ourselves as we hadn't yet. We'd actually be venturing into the town, with little idea who might be watching from any of the windows. Or who might come around a corner to spot us.

"Everything looks clear between us and them," I said, scanning the park and buildings ahead.

"We move together," Del said.

I nodded, and he left the cover of the dumpster first. I followed quickly, keeping up, with just ten feet separating us. For a guy in his mid-sixties with cancer eating at his bones, Del Drake was swift and sharp. He maneuvered from cover to cover. Using poles and signage to obscure our dash to the middle school. When we reached its corner, Del stopped us and took stock of the way ahead. Buildings lined the opposite side of the street. Empty buildings, we hoped, but couldn't be sure.

"We're damn exposed," I said.

"Yeah."

Twenty yards ahead the women now clung to each other on the ground, hugging and sobbing.

"Let's get them to come to us," Del said.

Rather than making a dash to where they sat just in front of the school's entrance alcove, we needed to draw their attention. And, quietly, urge them to move our way. It was all great in theory, but after what they'd just been through, there was no guarantee they'd have any trust toward men with guns.

Doubts aside, it was our best choice.

I fished around in the snow near the building with my gloved hand until I found what I was looking for—a rock. I leaned out past the corner of the building and hurled the chunk of stone toward the women, but not directly at them. It found its mark against the front side of the school and skidded off the brick façade with a stark scraping sound. The woman who hadn't been struck looked up at the impact. She was younger, I could see, maybe late twenties or early thirties, though with the physical hardships many had been through a true sense of age was more difficult to come by. The woman she'd shielded looked older, in her fifties, I gauged. The relationship and the situation began to gel in my mind. Daughter and mother, who'd just witnessed their father and husband being taken away. That was what we'd stumbled upon.

Del waved his hand as the younger woman looked our way. There was little chance she could not see us, but for a moment she did not react, simply holding herself frozen, gaze wide and wary.

I waved at her now, motioning with my hand to come in our direction. Now she did move, if only her head, swiveling to check her surroundings, much as the machine gunner had scanned for threats.

"Come on," I said, not loud, but also not hushed, urging her further with a more vigorous motion of my hand, practically windmilling it in the open.

The younger woman leaned toward the older woman, saying something, then she, too, looked at us.

"Come here," Del said, louder than I had.

The women stared at us for a moment, then looked to each other. Finally, the younger one helped the other up and they shuffled together up the sidewalk, moving our way, glancing behind every few seconds. There was true fear in their eyes. A look edging on terror. When they were only a few steps from us they stopped.

"You're not from here," the younger woman said.

"We want to talk to you," I said.

Del glanced across the street. A small office building sat on the corner there.

"Let's get inside," he said, looking to the women, their hesitance palpable. "We're not going to hurt you."

Again the women looked to each other, and the older one nodded. I stepped forward and slipped my arm under hers, helping as the four of us moved across the narrow street. Del reached the glass door of the office building first and pushed on it. It swung inward freely and we entered quickly.

I led the women away from the front door and into an empty office as Del searched the building, making sure we were secure within.

"My name is Eric," I told them, almost adding my last name, but quickly catching myself. Just as I'd stripped the license plates from my truck while fleeing to my refuge, lest the pursuing Trooper be able to identify me, here I wanted to share as little information as possible, not knowing how many records existed in town of 'Eric Fletcher' that would tie the name to my house in the woods.

"I'm Alicia Peterson," the younger woman said. "This is my mother, Lorraine."

"My friend is Del," I said, and he rejoined us from his survey of the building.

"We're pretty good here," he said, nodding to the women.

I did the introductions, then hesitated. Broaching what we'd witnessed would clearly be painful, but it was already that for these women.

"We saw what happened," I told them.

For a moment the 'what' didn't register. Then Lorraine settled into a chair in the office and buried her face in her hands, her daughter quickly leaning to put an arm around her mother.

"That was my father," Alicia said, confirming what we already suspected.

"Why did they take him?" Del asked.

"Because he couldn't work anymore," Alicia answered. "He was getting weaker. There isn't enough food, especially if you're working fourteen hours a day."

"Doing what?"

She puzzled at my question for a moment.

"You really don't know?"

"We're not from Whitefish," I said. "Tell us...what was he working on?"

"A bunker."

I looked to Del, my turn to be at a loss.

"He was working to build this for who?" Del asked. "Major Layton?"

Alicia nodded. Her mother calmed somewhat and looked up.

"He wasn't young anymore," Lorraine said, her voice cracking. "He couldn't keep up. That's why we brought him to the school."

"There was supposed to be a clinic open today for residents who needed treatment," Alicia explained.

"But it was a lie," Lorraine said. "A lie to get people who were sick or weak here to be taken. When we saw that no one else was showing up, we knew. We should have known better. I should have..."

She could say no more, and collapsed against her daughter, weeping again, unimaginable pain tearing at her.

"We wanted to get him help," Alicia said. "It's what's supposed to happen. People are supposed to help others. Right?"

She seemed as lost in the new reality as a newborn thrust into the world wailing and flailing, ripped from the warm comfort it had known. All was unknown and frightening.

"It's gotten worse the last two weeks," Alicia said. "Five people have been taken."

"People?" I pressed, keying in on the lack of specificity.

"One woman and four men," Alicia answered, then caught her mistake. "Five men now."

Her mother sobbed against her shoulder.

Shit...

I had to ask still more.

"Where do they take them?"

Alicia shrugged and shook her head. The not knowing had to be hell, I suspected.

"What about this bunker?" Del asked, redirecting the conversation. "What's it for? Where is it?"

"It's for the Major," Alicia said. "They're building it over at the field behind the high school. Digging down and reinforcing walls and, I don't know."

"What's it for?"

She thought on my question for a moment, her gaze narrowing down, as if this was yet another subject certain to bring pain.

"He hasn't said," Alicia told us, though that wasn't the end of her answer. "But some of his men have said he's building it so some can survive the cleanse."

"What the hell is that?" I asked, expecting no substantive answer, and receiving none.

"This Layton guy," Del began, looking to me. "He's sounding more cult leader than rogue military."

"Yeah," I agreed.

"What are you going to do?" Alicia asked.

"About what?" Del replied with his own question.

"The Major."

"We didn't come here to take on an army," Del told her. "No matter how puny."

"We need information," I explained, and her face reddened with simmering rage.

"So, you just come here to take what you want, for your own purposes, regardless of the effect it has on anybody else?" She looked between us, almost sneering the sudden hate she felt. "How the hell is that any different than what's he's doing?"

This wasn't our fight. Del and I both knew that. We'd made the conscious decision, separately, to keep to ourselves, trust few, and stay alive as long as possible. Engaging with a man who'd demonstrated a ruthless streak, along with a cadre of armed warriors at his beck and call, was beyond not only our intention, but also our ability.

"Listen, we can't—"

The roar of an engine accelerating cut me off. It was close, and drawing closer, coming from the north. Del broke away from the conversation and ran up the office stairs. I followed, the both of us carefully approaching the windows facing the rail yard. Beyond the glass we saw three more patrol vehicles, different than the others. These were smaller, basically SUV's that had had their roofs opened up. No machine guns were mounted, but an armed man stood tall in each hole, scanning the area as nine other men, three from each vehicle, congregated around the front of the museum, not far from the dumpster we'd taken cover behind.

"Dammit," Del swore, just as two of the men zeroed in on the tracks we'd made in the snow as we headed for the middle school.

"Not good," I said.

From below, the sound of the glass front door opening and then closing echoed upward, metal frame slapping metal jamb hard enough to reverberate through the structure. I shifted position, to a window overlooking the street between the office building and the middle school. Below I could see without difficulty Alicia and Lorraine running out into the street, moving with haste away from the building, both screaming something out and pointing back in our direction.

"They gave us up," Del said, and pointed to the far side of the upper floor. "Back stairs."

He led, knowing the way after his quick reconnaissance of the space a few minutes earlier, the throttled whine of engines racing fast rising as I followed, the both of us bounding down a narrow service staircase. At the bottom Del headed straight for a door at the end of a hallway, roughly opposite the one we'd come through when entering the building. We opened it and stepped into an alley, commotion sounding behind us, inside the office building we'd just left.

"Which way?" I asked Del.

"There," he said, pointing across the narrow alley to the back side of another building.

We tramped across the snowy ground, leaving more perfect tracks that would lead our pursuers right to us. Or would have, if Del hadn't stopped us at the back door to the building.

"Follow me," he said, shoving the door open and then, without entering, turning left and walking along the rear wall of the structure. "Stay close to the building."

I did as he was, our footsteps trampling the low drift of snow against the wall, but leaving no discernable trail. When we were beyond the corner of the building Del led us right, out of view, and down a narrow passage between a series of stores, the walkway here covered, the only trail behind us a non-specific mix of dirty slush mixed in with soil scattered from dead planter boxes. Someone had foraged here, hoping for some greenery to eat. Desperation, plain and simple.

Where the passage ended and spilled onto another street we paused, checking for any sign of life. There was none, but in the distance we could plainly hear shouts, and directives, those chasing us having found our back way out of the office building. The way clear, we ran across the street, stutter-stepping through a mix of tire tracks left by the patrol which had taken the husband and father from Lorraine and Alicia. On the far side we dashed through another mix of businesses, then past an apartment house and between what had once been quaint, compact houses.

"We have to get to the river," I said.

"My thought exactly," Del agreed.

The gunfire ahead of us turned that choice of destination to folly.

"Where now?"

Del considered my question. We were stuck between houses. People were shouting behind, from where we'd come. Ahead, some blocking force of armed individuals had taken up a position. Left was too deep into town. To the right was the rail yard, too wide open for a dash to freedom right then.

"There," Del said, pointing to a pair of rundown houses backing up to the rail yard. "That one."

I followed him across the narrow street, leaving a trail of tracks as we hurried to the house on the right.

"On the porch roof," Del directed me, and I climbed onto the porch railing, then hauled myself onto the small roof, an attic window just behind, glass and frame twisted off its mount.

"Here," Del passed his rifle up, but did not follow, turning instead back toward the front yard we'd just crossed.

A chorus of urgent voices grew. Closing in. To the west, between us and the river, more shots were fired, wild bursts, several rounds striking a power pole on the street corner. Wood splinters showered down.

"Get up here," I said, reaching down to Del, his plan, to seek cover in the attic, apparent now.

But he was already heading back to the street, retracing our steps, something long in his hand. A tree branch, dead and colorless, snapped from a leaning birch in the yard, itself nothing more than a dried length of wood waiting to topple. All the way to the far side of the street he ran, disappearing between the buildings, before emerging a moment later, dragging the branch behind, sweeping it back and forth, carving precise textures in the snow we'd trampled. From my vantage point above, I could see what he was doing—creating new, tiny drifts to match what already existed on the unused roadway, masking the trail we'd left. He wielded the branch like a sculptor, backing toward the house, erasing his own tracks until he stood below again.

"Come on!" I urged him.

More shots cracked close. And the voices, urgent before, were now near frantic, like some pack of dogs closing in on their prey. Del tossed the branch back beneath the tree and climbed onto the porch railing. I took his hand and pulled him up, both of us slipping through the small attic window and into the dark space. The last through, I passed our weapons to Del and pulled the attic window until it was secure.

As soon as it clicked into place, a half dozen men appeared across the street, staring at the ground. I eased back from the filthy window and did nothing but breathe for the next ten minutes.

Twenty Six

"They're gone," I whispered to Del as I watched from our attic perch, my face to one side of the window, peering out at an angle I hoped would obscure me. Hoped.

"About damn time," he said quietly.

The half dozen men had turned to two dozen, all pouring over the area where we'd disappeared, any hope of finding remnants of our tracks ended after the first few ran about wildly, charging across lawns and into houses. Including the one in which we had secreted ourselves. For five minutes they'd banged around below before bashing through the attic access with the butts of their rifles. At least one had poked his head into the space and shined a light back and forth, but Del and I were tucked away behind piles of insulation and a low support wall for a dormer at the rear of the house. When they finally left the house we could hear them even down the block, doing a similar number on the abandoned houses there.

Now, hours later, with night falling, it seemed that they had either moved on to seek us elsewhere, or given up on the search entirely. Still, we hadn't moved more than a few feet inside the cramped attic, crawling on hands and knees when shifting positions. Waiting. For what, we hadn't yet decided.

"Are we reevaluating this visit to Whitefish yet?" I asked, joking

"I don't know about you, but I am going to write a strongly worded letter to their chamber of commerce."

I chuckled. Darkness was settling beyond the window. Minus the minor glow of distant stars and the sliver of moon, it would be total. The new world, nearly powerless, was a stargazer's delight. It gave me a chance to take in the blackening heavens through the window. Time to take a breath. Time to think.

The latter was not entirely a pleasant endeavor.

"What do you think they did with the man?"

Del looked at me, just enough light left to make it plain I suspected an answer to my own question.

"Are you wondering why they didn't just work him to death?"

I nodded. It was a half lie masquerading as agreement.

"You want me to say it so you can just stop thinking it?"

What I'd seen in Eureka, next to the makeshift fire on the sidewalk, was at the forefront of what I considered the truth here to be. The terrible, terrible truth.

Still, I couldn't say it.

"Work a man to death," Del began, "you work the meat right off of him."

"These people are cattle to Major Layton," I said, hating the man I'd never laid eyes upon.

"And slaves," Del reminded me. "That's why he needs people here—to build that bunker for whatever that 'cleansing' bullshit is."

I nodded. But only briefly. The spot of harsh white on the underside of the roof beyond Del drew my attention away from our exchange. The soft rumble building beneath and all around then pulled Del away from the subject we'd danced around.

"What the hell is that?" I asked.

"That sounds like..."

He didn't have to finish. Together we began to move, crawling across the joists until we were at the rear attic dormer, a window set into it, blazing white light spilling through. We eased close to the portal, making sure there was no one outside and below to spot us, and looked out across the rail yard to a trio of locomotives dragging a long train of tank cars to a stop well past the Baker Avenue Bridge.

"Interesting," Del said. "Any ideas on what to make of this?"

I wondered that myself as we watched groups of men approach the lead locomotive, greeting others as they disembarked from the still rumbling diesel behemoth.

"Food oils are transported by train," I suggested. "Corn, canola."

It was a halfhearted offering at best, and convinced neither of us. Del took out his binoculars and dialed in the scene at the lead locomotive. I did the same with my more compact pair.

"Smiling faces," Del observed. "Handshakes, back slapping."

I saw it, too. But I also saw something else. Approaching from the east.

"Three vehicles coming," I said.

Del shifted his view and watched with me as the trio of cars, not pickups or SUVs, sped toward the head of the train, bright rooster tails of snow kicked up in their wake. As they neared the locomotive, all attention of those already there turned to the new arrivals. Each car stopped, a mix of men and women exiting, all armed.

All but one.

"Hello, Major Layton," Del said softly.

The unarmed man strode directly toward the locomotive crew and greeted them warmly. He wore no sign proclaiming his name or rank, just a dark brown parka and a mile-wide smile. But all about him screamed authority. His gait. The deference paid to him by those near. He was someone special to these people, and, from what we'd gleaned, only one man fit that description.

"You'd think these guys just delivered the Stanley Cup to their hometown mayor," I said.

"They did something right, that's for sure."

The love fest at the front of the train ended, Layton and his entourage walking back along the track, past the locomotives, to the first of the tank cars. Flashlights came on and swept across the numbering on the bulbous carrier.

"Any idea what the numbers mean?" Del asked.

"None," I answered. "I bet they know."

Layton and his people continued back several cars, giving each a quick look, before congregating again. They talked for several minutes, the leader making a few hand gestures, toward the lake, I thought, or beyond. Then he shook hands again and returned to his car, which pulled fast away, the other two that had come with it departing as well. The train crew and those who had greeted them on foot walked together back to the lead engine and continued their conversation.

I lowered my binoculars, as did Del, the both of us looking to the other.

"We should be able to make it out of here when it's full dark," he said, that condition probably less than ten minutes away.

"Yeah," I concurred, but without much enthusiasm.

We had to leave. If the chance presented itself, it was the smart move to get out of Whitefish and back to our homes. But, at the moment, all I felt, all both of us felt, was that we'd come to this place seeking answers, but would be leaving with even more unanswered questions.

Twenty Seven

We skirted the bank of the iced-over river and worked our way north from Whitefish, hugging the western shore of the lake, stopping wherever cover existed again and again. We heard occasional patrols nearby as far north as Dog Bay, just outside of town. Beyond that the night's light wind was the only sound.

We reached our homes after midnight, Del trudging off to his along the path through the dead woods. I returned to my refuge with the intention of sleeping. The two way trip to Whitefish, and the exertion, both physical and mental, that we'd endured while there, felt as though it had sapped my energy down to the bone. All I wanted was to collapse.

But I didn't. I couldn't. Thoughts of Whitefish, of its people, or what its people had once been, grated on me. I was boiling down the entirety of what the blight had wrought upon the whole of the world to this one town in northern Montana. How many other Whitefishes were out there? How many places of horror? How many Major Laytons?

That was what scared me, truly. If somehow I survived, if the plants and the trees and the crops staged a slow comeback at some point, would places like Whitefish be all there was to seek beyond my refuge? Would all gatherings of people have devolved into a similar state?

If that turned out to be the case, then surviving would seem a grand folly.

I couldn't sleep. Not yet. Not with those cheery musings on my mind. I sat in my great room, the hearth cold, as was the space around it. The warmth I'd know this night waited in my bedroom, the electric blanket I'd had to kill for wired exactly as Del's was. The chill, though, did not drive me from my place on the couch. I watched my breath, misty puffs in the cold, then reached for the remote and turned the TV on.

The Denver station spat static at me. Electronic noise. But, in that, I saw hope. I was reminded of hope. People there had broken through the Red Signal. They'd persevered. Shined a light on what was happening. For a while.

But now they were gone. Piled in a heap with their loved ones by the side of the road, maybe. I'd seen that. Or, reduced to nourishment for the stronger. I'd seen that, too.

"Enough," I said aloud, to myself, for myself.

I was going to a dark place. Because I'd just come from a dark place. Just *escaped* from a dark place.

This was my home. My refuge. There was no darkness here.

"No darkness," I repeated my own thinking. "No darkness."

A few minutes later, slumped into the deep cushions of my couch, sleep took me, to its own dark place.

* * *

"—so she just walked into the fire."

I was dreaming. A hearing dream, with no images to fill the canvas of my drowsing mind.

"She never twitched, never flinched."

Where was the vision being described? Why was I not—

"The fire embraced her and took her and she let it."

My eyes opened, leaving no dream behind, because there had been none. There had only been what I saw before me on the television screen—the near hollow shell of a man staring at me from the anchor desk in Denver.

"She set the fire, and let it take her."

Lights flickered behind the man. The image of him fuzzed, then stabilized. Power on his end was tenuous, it seemed, but he was coming through. The station was broadcasting again, monitors on the wall behind and above him all static but one, a solid red rectangle filling it.

"She wouldn't go with me," the man said, his voice seeming faint, the small microphone laying on the desk before him too distant for perfect clarity. "I wanted to go a different way."

I lifted myself from where I'd tilted onto the couch when falling asleep, sitting now to watch the man, wishing there was some way to reach Del quickly. To have him join me. But the age of instant, ubiquitous communication was past. There was no DVR to record this broadcast. Leaving to get my friend might only result in the both of us returning to find static again. I had to stay, and watch.

Then I realized it—I might be the only one seeing this.

"I worked here," the man said, letting his gaze play over parts of the studio the camera did not reveal. He lifted an emaciated arm, sleeve of a coat seeming to hang on bone alone, and pointed up to his right. "Over there, in the control room."

He smiled. Not just some weak expression to match his physical state, but a true, beaming smile filled with memory and happiness and longing.

"Right up there," he said, his hand coming down to join the other still hidden beneath the desk. "You can run this whole place from right there. Turn the cameras on and come down here and pretend you're Jim Winters."

Jim Winters...

I wondered where he was. A man I'd never met, didn't know, but who became, with his colleagues, narrators of the world beyond my refuge as it descended into the abyss.

"Jim was a good guy," the man said.

Was...

This man, did he have some knowledge of Jim Winters' fate? Or was his choice of verbiage just the norm now. Everyone 'was'. There were few who were still 'is'. Past tense ruled the new world.

"He was at our wedding," the man said, no trace of the grand smile he'd flashed remaining. No wistful hint of it. He looked straight into the camera. Right at me. "She chose fire. I don't know why. I wish she'd gone with me. It won't be long now."

That was when the man brought his other hand out from beneath the desk and lifted it to look at the blood dripping from his wrist.

"No..." I said at the sight.

He stood from the chair behind the anchor desk and steadied himself with his good hand atop the flat surface. Blood soaked the left sleeve of his dark coat, the hand at the end looking as if it had been dipped in red paint.

"She should have come with me," the man said. "No pain. No pain at all."

He stepped away from the desk, letting go of his handhold, and wobbled off camera, still speaking, the microphone registering nothing but wispy mumbles as the distance increased. I stared at the screen, waiting for the stranger to reappear, but he didn't. For the next two days I watched the station on and off, until, in the afternoon on a Friday, the lights in the studio dimmed and the broadcast went to static. Likely the generator powering the station had run out of fuel, sputtering to a stop. How the man had managed to get the generator and the station up and running in his condition was almost miraculous.

Determination was how, I knew. His overriding need to make some last statement. A valediction breathed out to a world mostly gone, with no certainty that it would be known.

That was one of the true horrors the blight had wrought. Where a big enough rock dropping from space would have made everyone's exit from this life mostly comparable, this slow motion unraveling of humanity, often one soul at a time, seemed only to hint at what lay ahead for those who were still hanging on.

What sort of hell had the woman this man spoke of, presumably his wife, endured to bring her to a place where in immolation she saw peace and release.

Hell on earth was real. I wanted to tell myself things were going to get better. But I couldn't.

A few days after what I watched on the Denver station, Del noticed me staring off and asked what my brain was chewing on. I hadn't told him of what I'd seen, and I crafted an innocuous lie to mask what I was really thinking—how I would end my life if I found myself in a place, a state of being, known by the man in Denver and untold numbers of others, anonymous to me, and to history.

Part Four

Maelstrom

Twenty Eight

Spring whimpered into the north of the state, colorless and cold, drenching rains replacing bouts of heavy snow that had kept Del and me from doing much of anything other than popping in on each other two or three times a week. There'd been no more treks to Whitefish, and only a few hikes longer than a mile or two, mostly to scout houses and cabins between us and town, several of those that were easily accessible by road showing traps set similar to what Del had found at Eddie Martin's getaway. The ones we could we disarmed, taking the TNT with us. Others, though, remained as dangerous as we'd found them, but, to date, no blast had echoed through the valley. No wayward refugee, from Whitefish or elsewhere, had stumbled upon the empty homes.

The most interesting thing we heard, though, as one season changed to another, was not the crack of a trap that had finally paid off for Major Layton, but the throaty, thumping growl of a diesel locomotive heading north. That one or more of the engines the Major had procured was heading up the tracks was interesting enough. That it stopped compelled Del and me to investigate further.

We headed north first, wanting to gain a view of the rail line from somewhere not in the vicinity of our land. Thirty minutes into our trek, while our view of the highway and the rail line that paralleled it was obscured by terrain, we heard the locomotive throttle up again, the sound receding as it seemed to head back south. Sixty more minutes of quickened hiking brought us to an elevation where we could see without impairment miles of track and highway. Neither of us needed our binoculars to see that the locomotive had left something behind.

A tank car.

"I'm thinking our friend the Major has some grand plan in mind," Del said.

"Or he's littering in an extreme way."

Del chuckled. But only for a moment, a seriousness descending quickly.

"He's also into setting traps," Del reminded.

I hadn't considered that. We could be looking at a multi-ton hunk of bait hoping to draw us out. A carrot dangled before a rabbit. The Major and his men knew their security had been penetrated. Worse, they knew we'd evaded every pursuer thrown at us. The most they might have been able to discern was that our direction of travel was generally north.

Right where they'd left the tank car.

"If that's the case, then we're not the only ones watching," I said.

Del and I backed away from our vantage point and took a circuitous path back to our homes, giving the possible trap as wide a berth as possible.

Twenty Nine

The two days following our discovery of the tank car, we heard no more sounds hinting at another locomotive chugging through the mountains. Or rather, I didn't.

Del hadn't stopped by, and hadn't been at his house when I'd made the hike to look in on him. Nothing seemed amiss. His house was secure. Still, there was reason to worry. If the tank car had been placed as a trap to lure us out, it was conceivable that one or more of Major Layton's men had reconnoitered the area and stumbled upon Del, either in his house or outside. I wasn't conceding this as a likelihood, but I couldn't fully discount it.

I reminded myself that, in the months I'd known Del, he often trekked off on his own, scouting his domain, and, I believed, communing with what was left of nature. At one time, in the old world, I imagine that he wandered about the lush woods frequently. To smell the trees. Take in the sight of God's creatures. Sip from cool, clear streams. None of that existed anymore. The woods were dead, as were the animals who'd called them home. Creeks were fouled with the blight's decay, foliage of every kind being slowly reduced to an ashen dust that was carried on the wind, or sluiced along drainages to choke waterways. Del might very well be out there now, despite the waste that had spread upon the land.

That's what I believed. That's what I told myself for the next two days. But after five days gone, it became apparent that something was wrong.

Early on the sixth day I loaded a pack and headed out to look for my friend. I had no indications to go on. No idea at all where he might have gone, or what might have motivated him to go. His rifle was not in his house, nor was the small pack he took with him on day treks. In it he usually stored some food, a flimsy shelter that went up quickly and was better than being left in the elements, though not by much, and other essentials. Beyond that, Del had expressed a belief that, even after the blight, a man had most things in nature that he needed to survive.

I believed my friend could survive if he'd fallen ill, or been injured. If he'd been taken, that was another matter.

My plan was to work a search area in expanding circles, with Del's house as the center. Every rotation I'd shift outward a hundred yards or so. It would take hours for the immediate few rounds. And days more, if I found nothing to guide me to somewhere beyond that closer area.

As it was, eight hours after beginning, I found the first hint that something had gone terribly wrong.

The body lay behind a cluster of small trees that would never know maturity. Rocks and fallen branches had been piled hastily over the man's corpse and dirt kicked over his boots in an attempt to conceal him. Without difficulty I could tell that it was not Del. I could also see that the man's throat had been cut, a deep slice below the jaw line, what had spilled crusted over his face and upper body. He was swelling, decomposition setting in. I was no coroner, but I had seen the various stages of animal decay in the wild. If the human body broke down at anything close to those rates, I could guess that the man had laid here, unmolested by scavengers that had long since gone the way of other forest dwellers, for three or four days.

Then I saw what lay next to him, partially concealed by the branches and dirt and the left side of his body—a rifle. An AK-47, magazine still its well, bolt forward. I slowly swung my AR from where it had hung behind and took it in hand, setting the safety to *fire*. It might have been several days since this man met his fate, but I had no idea who had taken him out, or who he was. One of Layton's men? If so, why was he here?

No answers existed where I stood, so I began to search the immediate area. Looking for signs of a struggle. Tracks. Anything pointing to the direction the victor in this confrontation had taken.

Two hundred yards away I found another body.

This man lay face down, in the open, an AK nearly identical to the other a few yards away in the dirt. Lying as if tossed away, or lost in some struggle.

And a struggle there had been. All around the man there were gouges in the forest floor where boots had dug in. A sapling was bent, its thin trunk snapped. The man's back was covered by a coat with three penetrations, each about two inches across, thin like the blade of a knife, the area around each soaked dark. He'd been taken from behind.

I crouched and scanned the area. There was no immediate sign of anyone or anything else. Including Del.

And then I began to wonder—had Del done this?

Distance is your friend...

Yes, it most certainly was, but here the killing had been up close and personal. The wounds, on this man especially, matched the menacing blade that Del carried on his belt. I kept one hand on my AR and used the other to grip the man's shoulder, rolling him to his back. His dead eyes, bulging and black, looked like shadows searching for some heaven above. On the ground where he'd lain, a knife was half buried in the dirt, blade planted deep. I pulled it free and examined the blade, thin and narrow. It was not the one that had caused his wounds. More than likely, it was his, and he'd fallen on it when the life bled out of him during the fight.

But he hadn't gone down completely vanquished. Caked to the dirty blade was a smear of red. His own defensive strike, or strikes, had found some mark.

I dropped the knife and stood quickly, my worry tripling instantly.

"Del!" I shouted, unconcerned with the possibility of alerting anyone. Two dead bodies lay in the relative open. If anyone was near, they would have stumbled upon what I had. "Del!"

I listened, then moved down the slope and to the west, just twenty yards, to a jumble of smooth rocks rising from the earth, and climbed atop, looking out in every direction.

"Del!"

Again, I heard nothing. But I did see something—the slender barrel of a rifle being lifted in the air, pointing skyward.

Del's rifle.

I jumped from the rocks and ran down and across the leaning side of the hill, to a shallow depression just above a bubbling creek. Del lay there, curled against the side, mud-caked poncho wrapping him, his face pale, lips blue.

"Hey neighbor," he said, then collapsed as he tried to stand.

Thirty

"The first one I saw about sundown," Del said. "His buddy came looking for him a little after dark."

Del half lay on his couch, shifting for a comfortable position. I'd carried him home the day before, cleaning and doing some Frankenstein stitches on a long gash just above his hip. He'd lost a fair amount of blood, but had the sense to get the cut packed off with a piece of his shirt. That, and the five cold nights he'd endured, might have slowed his metabolism and, despite the threat of hypothermia, saved his life. For the past few hours I'd been practically force feeding him, making him eat and drink to begin replenishing his strength.

"The second fella was a helluva lot more to handle than the first," Del explained. "I had the drop on him. Did a quick grab and slice across his throat before he could get a scream out."

"The guy had to be half your age," I marveled.

"I had the tactical advantage with him. The other one, I wasn't so lucky."

I nodded—*no shit*.

"I tried to rush him from behind and upslope. I had the momentum, but all my first strike did was knock his rifle out of his hand. We fell and rolled, got up, he pulled a knife, and it was on."

"How'd you get him in the back?"

"He slipped on that slope," Del said, shaking his head. "When he came up I was behind him. Got an arm around his neck and got my strikes in. Then he did this wild behind the back haymaker with his knife and got me. By then, the fight was pretty much out of him. He just folded and did a face plant."

"You crazy son of a bitch," I said.

"Listen, I would have preferred to shoot them. But then I didn't know how many of their buddies I'd have running toward the sound of gunfire."

I made a mental note that, despite adding some unwieldy length to the weapon, I'd mount the suppressor I had on my AR whenever I ventured out. Being able to quiet any shot would have served Del well in his encounter.

"Turned out is was just the two of them on that hill."

"How are you sure about that?"

"After I put the second guy down, I followed their tracks back to—"

"Wait," I interrupted. "You were stabbed. You were hurt. And you went off looking for more trouble?"

"I didn't know how bad I was hurt," Del said. "But I found their transportation down off an old logging road, maybe half a mile from where I ambushed them. It was one of those four wheel dealies like you have."

"An ATV?"

He nodded, then grabbed a hunk of reconstituted chicken from the plate on the coffee table. He ate it in two bites, his appetite encouraging.

"Just big enough for the two of them," Del said. "I rolled it down and over into the ravine. No one's going to find it there. By the time I was done with that and heading back up the hill, well, it started to hit me how bad I was hurt."

"You should have fired off a shot then," I told him. "I would have heard."

"So would anyone else out there," Del reminded me. "I didn't know if it was just these two, or if they were spread out on different roads looking for us."

He had a rock solid point. If our supposition was correct.

"How sure are you that these guys were sent by the Major?"

"Because before I took action, I watched, and I listened. The guy I gave the permanent smile to was grumbling to himself that if Layton wanted the two intruders so bad he should be out looking himself."

That settled it. We were being actively hunted.

"So they're not just waiting to bait us out with that tank car," I said.

Del eased himself up, sitting now, an uncertain expression rising.

"Yeah," he began. "I think we were wrong about that."

"How so?"

"The day I went out scouting, I saw another tank car about a mile down the track toward Whitefish. Parked just like the one near us. I decided to look a little further."

"And?"

"There's more. Spaced about every mile along the track south of here. I was on my way back to tell you when I crossed paths with those two."

I tried to analyze the reasons they might have scattered the tank cars. Some possibilities were quite disturbing.

"There's a good chance whatever's in those things is dangerous," I suggested. "Layton might not want it concentrated near town."

"He had the damn things dragged right into town," Del said.

"Could be fuel he's going to try to filter or process to be usable. Some chemical for something."

"Dangerous shit all around," Del commented.

We had no answer that satisfied either of us. And we had more immediate concerns, primary among those being getting Del healthy.

"No more damn scouting missions on your own," I said.

"You're not old enough or pretty enough to mother me."

I laughed. So did my friend. It was a light moment, and the both of us savored it like the rarity it was.

Thirty One

I filled a mug with steaming coffee and placed it on the table in front of Del.

"I do miss this," Del said, lifting the cup and sampling the aroma for a long moment before taking a sip. He'd stopped by, mostly to assure me that he was all right after his scare in the woods the previous week. "The smell, you know? There's just something about that smell. The slightly bitter roast of the beans."

"You talk about coffee like some people do about wine," I said, and sat at the kitchen table across from the closest thing I had to a friend and confidant. In actuality, I realized, he was that. And more. Nearly losing him in a chance encounter with a pair of Layton's men was, still, difficult to get past. "But we'll both be missing it for good soon."

Del understood.

"Supply getting down there?"

I nodded. Between the theft and some spoilage due to cans with bad seals, I had recalculated the length of the time I had before the reality of starvation came knocking. A few months, if I didn't cut back. The last grounds of coffee I'd just used were inconsequential compared to dwindling supply of calories.

"How about the rest of your stores?"

"I was hoping some elk might have pulled through," I said, not wanting to alarm Del. I was beginning to fear, even with the threat of my food running out, that I would still outlive him. His walk was more tentative than ever, pain obvious. Somewhere inside, the cancer was running amok.

"Keep hoping."

One elk could feed me for months. But that would require the elk to have a food source, which none had. Not for months. Still, Del and I had survived. Could some game, if not elk specifically, have also hung on? It was a chance. A long shot. But survival these days was edging toward equal portions luck and preparation.

"Something might have pulled through. Bear feeding on carrion." Enough other species had dropped dead from starvation to provide a buffet for some sturdy grizzlies. "If the weather breaks soon I might give it a try to the west a ways."

"It's funny," Del said, actually smiling after a sip of coffee. "We used to count on some voice on the radio, or some fat guy on TV to tell us how long a storm would last. Or if one was coming at all. Now..."

"Yeah," I agreed.

"We've lost most of the ability to sense things like the weather," Del said. He drank for a moment, seeming to get lost in some thought before looking to me again. "Some have lost more sense than that."

"Our friend the Major?"

Del shook his head, dismissing the man with visible derision.

"He's a wannabe dictator," Del said. "And the rest..."

"They're confused and scared."

"No," Del disagreed, not buying my appraisal of those who remained in Whitefish. "Layton is killing them slowly. There's a time to put your life on the line to stand up to scum like him. For those folks, the time has passed." He drank the last of the coffee I'd poured him. "If I had a nuke and a plane, I'd turn that town and everyone in it to glass."

He set the empty cup on the table and gave an odd half smile.

"That's just me," Del said. "I figure we've gone a long time accommodating people in this world who let evil exist, even flourish, all around them, because they claim fear. But if you let fear rule you, you enable the one who dishes it out. That's how evil grows. That's how it spreads."

"All that is necessary for evil to triumph is that good men do nothing?"

I related the famed quotation as a question. Del smiled and nodded.

"Exactly."

"You'd wipe out a town to get Layton?" I asked, still unsure of how to reconcile the absolute of Del's belief with the kind man I'd come to know.

"That town is Layton now," Del said. "You saw those women turn on us, even after watching their man get taken away to get chopped up for steaks."

"Like I said, they were afraid."

Del leaned forward, planting his elbows on the table and laying a hard look on me. Maybe even harsh.

"Would you let him do what he's doing if you lived in that town?"

"I'd probably be dead," I said.

"For standing up to him?"

I nodded.

"That good men do nothing," Del recited. "You're a good man. That town is out of good men, or women."

I took Del's empty cup and put it in the sink. The scent of coffee still lingered in the air. All that would remain after its fleeting presence was memory. A memory forever linked with this conversation with my friend.

"I'm gonna head home," Del said, standing and heading for the back door, his hand patting me gently on the back as he passed. "Thanks for sharing the last of your coffee."

He took his rifle from next to the door and left. I watched him through the kitchen windows as he disappeared into the bare, colorless woods, reaching to trees as he passed, grabbing handholds to support his failing form.

* * *

I was lost in a dream of a place I'd never been when pounding rocked me from sleep. Hazy mental images of green-blue water curling onto a white sand beach were scattered as my eyes snapped open and I reached for my rifle, covers flying off. For an instant I was terrified that the raiders had returned. Until a voice rose with the slamming of a fist against my back door.

Del's voice.

"Turn on your TV," he said as I let him in.

I did as he said. The static of the Denver station filled the screen.

"Nothing, see?"

"Try another station."

"This was a bootleg setup," I told him. "I was lucky to get that station out of the Rockies."

"You think any subscriber protocols are still being enforced?"

He had a point. But there was still the Red Signal to muck up any broadcast.

Or so I thought.

I scanned through the satellite feed, getting only static, until I reached what should be CNN. No logo appeared on the static-free transmission, but, more importantly, neither was there any large red rectangle. Just some antiquated color bar test pattern showed on screen.

"The Red Signal..."

"It's gone," Del said. "Radio frequencies are clear, too."

I was surprised there was any signal coming from CNN. But, then, it might not even be from them. It could simply be a placeholder image the satellite was feeding to ground receivers like mine.

"Did you hear anything?"

He looked at me and nodded.

"You should probably hear it, too."

* * *

I followed Del along the trail to his house and into his radio room. The equipment was already on, speaker spewing static, until...

"Come back if you are in the Kalispell or Whitefish area."

The transmission was near crystal clear. I looked to Del.

"I flipped the thing on, like I do a couple times a day, just to see if that idiotic signal was still broadcasting, but it wasn't." He sat at the only chair and reached toward one of the radios, adjusting a dial. "So I fished around seeing if I could pick up anything, and I heard this."

"Any survivors in the Kalispell or Whitefish areas, you must report in."

I looked to Del. He'd keyed in on the same thing.

"Must," Del repeated. "How's that for a friendly greeting?"

We listened to the silence for a moment.

"Three possibilities," Del said. "No one's listening. No one cares."

"Or no one is left," I finished for my friend.

"Survivors, you are ordered to report in by authority of territorial executive Major James Layton. Report in now."

Del nodded and looked to me.

"He's still at it. And he likes giving orders."

"You inclined to follow that order?" I asked, already knowing the answer.

"No. But I am inclined to find out more about this Major. A helluva lot more."

"If you're thinking of a return visit to Whitefish..."

My resistance to that possibility was plain. Del turned the radio off and stood.

"I'm thinking we bring the fight to them," Del said, grinning. "Or them to the fight."

Some idea was percolating in the man's crafty brain.

"I say we issue an invitation," Del said. "And welcome them with open arms."

For the next hour we formulated a plan. Three days later we had everything in place and were ready to take decisive action.

Thirty Two

Del and I watched the cabin from a hill sixty yards away, concealed behind a knot of felled trees wedged over a sizeable boulder.

"I heard something last night," Del said. "Something odd."

I puzzled at his out-of-the-blue statement. He'd mentioned nothing of this on our two hours hiking to our present location. In fact, thinking on it, Del had been unusually quiet. I'd thought the lack of conversation was due to some serious reflection on the action we were about to take

"What did you hear?"

"I couldn't sleep, so I turned on my radio. I've done that for years. Back before all this, I'd tune into some far off station and start up a conversation with a total stranger. Might talk for twenty, thirty minutes. Just jabbering. Now, I have to resist the urge to hit that transmit button." He nodded, mostly to himself. "I really had to resist that last night."

I'd thought Del might have been woken by a strange sound outside. An animal that had survived. Or intruders. It appeared, though, that what was troubling him came from somewhere distant. Somewhere unknown.

"So I just listened," Del went on. "To static, mostly. Then I happened upon a station right at the end of its transmission. All I heard was 'This is Eagle One, signing off.'"

"Eagle One?"

Del nodded.

"Signal was clear as day. There was some serious wattage behind that station."

"Eagle One," I said again. "Is that call sign anything special? I mean, you hear *Eagle This* or *Eagle That* and it sounds potentially official. Like some military or governmental thing. Even presidential."

"Yeah," Del said.

Del was as subdued as I'd ever seen him. This thing he'd heard really had its hooks in him. Why, I hadn't a clue.

"It was just someone talking," I reminded him.

"No," he countered. "You don't understand. The voice...it was a boy. It was a kid."

A kid...

That threw me for a moment. It was hardly likely that a child somewhere was unscathed by the blight. But a child surviving implied an adult had along with them. We knew there were people out there. People like us who had hung on. But, if Del had heard right, a child somewhere had access to a working radio with abundant power supplying it.

"Any idea how old?"

"Not that old," Del said. "I used to talk to teenage hams all over the country, even the world. This was no teen."

"Eagle One," I said yet again, as if its repetition would somehow inform me as to its meaning.

"I'm going to listen in tonight around the same time," Del said.

"Just listen, right?"

He hesitated. In the few days since the Red Signal ended, Del had heard a few distant stations calling out. All desperate. Most operated by people who'd happened upon a radio with some sort of working power source and were simply crying out like a child might at night, begging for help, pleading for food, supplies, protection. And he'd only allowed himself to listen. Hadn't transmitted once.

But I could tell he was thinking about it.

"I could listen with you," I said.

"Hold my hand?" Del asked, humoring me.

"Behind your back."

He smiled, relaxing a bit. The both of us looked back to the cabin. We'd been watching it for an hour, just to ensure no one else was near. When we were satisfied we ducked behind the heft of the boulder and Del touched the loose end of the wire to the spare ATV battery we'd lugged over, energizing the circuit, the charge ripping through the remainder of the length and reaching the blasting caps. The caps, mini explosives themselves, detonated just milliseconds after Del sent the charge down the wire, their explosion setting off the three sticks of TNT bundled together in the crawlspace beneath the cabin.

In an instant the structure was obliterated. Lumber and tile and furniture and ductwork and everything else contained by the four walls was launched skyward and sprayed out, jagged lengths of splintered two-by-four impaling dead pines. Twisted shards of metal from the cabin's stove and an old claw foot bathtub chopped through desiccated branches above, the pulverized wood turned to powder and chunky grit. Smoldering bits of wood and paneling arced hundreds of feet through the woods, sparking small fires that struggled to smolder on the storm dampened slopes. Debris from the blast spun and tumbled aloft until gravity pulled it earthward, showering the landscape, bits of the home that had been whole just seconds earlier thudding to earth around Del and me. We hugged the back of the sturdy rock until the air seemed clear of debris, then we leaned to look past the obstacle.

The buried foundation of the cabin poked from the earth, smoldering, licks of flame slowly devouring the thick timber supports, a long column of grey and white smoke filtering past the bare pines and drifting into the morning sky like a marker screaming *something happened here!* to anyone within fifty miles.

That was exactly what we were hoping for.

* * *

It took us fifteen minutes after the blast to prepare for what we hoped would happen next, then we split up. Del moved west about a hundred yards to a position where he could see the narrow lane that allowed access to the otherwise remote cabin. I remained behind the boulders, my suppressed AR ready.

We only had to wait an hour.

The lone pickup rolled to a stop just in front of the destroyed structure. Three men piled out of the cab, and three from the open bed, no machinegun mounted on this truck. They held their arms casually and laughed, admiring the destruction they believed their trap had caused. One made a comment about searching for chunks. Another reminded that Layton wanted something to display, no doubt as a concrete warning to those who might seek shelter beyond the town.

I listened for just a moment before reaching for the battery. We'd run new wires after the initial explosion, and placed what we'd already prepared for the maximum intended effect. One of the wires was already connected. The other lay on the ground. I picked it up and ducked fully behind the boulders again and touched it to the battery terminal.

The explosion this time came not from below, but from above, three sticks of TNT, each lashed ten feet up on separate trees, the blast surrounding the rubbled cabin on three sides, pressure wave from each snapping the trees they were tied to and rushing outward, slamming into the unsuspecting patrol sent from Whitefish.

I popped up just as the concussion subsided, taking aim through my tactical scope. Three men appeared to be dead outright. Another was rolling on the ground and reaching for his rifle. He got a hand on it as a shot rang out, Del firing from up the road, his aim threading through the trees to take that man down with a round to the chest. Another man already had his weapon in hand and was shaking off the blast, raising it in the direction Del's shot had come from. I placed the glowing triangle in my sight on the side man's side and squeezed off two fast shots, only one impacting as he moved, driving in one side of his skull and exiting out the other in a chunky mist the color and texture of ripe watermelon. He crumpled into an unnatural heap, one arm bent at an impossible angle.

The last man had the most brains among his comrades and ignored the weapon that had been blasted from his grip. He scurried away from the house and was just getting to his feet to run for the road when I fired, my aim purposely low. The single shot found its mark in the back of his thigh and he fell, rolling toward the downslope beyond the demolished house.

The man had pulled himself to a sitting position, back against a tree. His sole weapon, an AR like mine but fitted with a hideously unreliable drum magazine, lay a dozen yards from him, far beyond any reconsideration of abandonment. He made hardly a move or sound at all as Del and I approached.

"What's your name?" I asked.

The man looked up at us, both hands pressed hard against a wound on the front of his thigh. The wound I'd given him. Blood bubbled past his fingers.

"Your name," I repeated.

Now the man glanced to his rifle. Del backed away and picked it up, heaving it down the slope beyond the trees before returning to his place with me. I shifted the aim of my AR until its suppressed muzzle was pointed at the man's nose.

"Hank Coggins," he finally replied.

I lowered my aim.

"Where are you from, Hank?"

He looked between us again, reality setting in. This was not chit chat—it was an interrogation. And he was a prisoner.

"Boise."

"You're a long way from home," Del said.

Hank winced, pain from his wound spiking. His face bore cuts from shrapnel tossed by the blast, and the left side of his coat was shredded, likely by the same. Beneath the tattered garment I could see more blood, a wide smear of it sliding down and over his hip, staining the tan work pants he wore.

"Who is the Major?" I asked. "Where is he from?"

"What do you mean?" Hank asked, genuinely confused.

"Where the hell did he get the rank from?" Del pressed the man, forceful and impatient.

"I don't know," Hank said. "I met up with him over in Coeur d'Alene. He was looking for men, and he had food, transportation."

"Okay," Del said, dialing the menace in his voice up a notch. "What the hell brought him to Whitefish?"

"I think he grew up here," Hank answered, his body seeming to press into the tree and away from Del. "I never heard it from him. Just from others who were closer to him. Folks who'd been with him since the shit hit the fan."

"He's not Army, Guard, anything?" I asked.

"I don't know. Honest. I don't know shit."

That might actually be true, I knew. But we were going to make damn sure of it.

"What the hell is with the tank cars?" I asked.

"What do you mean?"

Del drew his rifle back, wielding the butt, ready to lay a blow down on the reluctant prisoner. Hank recoiled, shrinking down, bringing a bloodied hand up to defend himself against the threatened strike.

"I don't know what you mean!" Hank protested as Del held the rifle back and ready, like a coiled snake. "All right! All right! Don't hurt me!"

"Why did he put them out along the track?" I demanded. "What's in them?"

A cough rattle from Hank's mouth. His chest shuddered, and he gulped air. The hand that had risen as a shield lowered again and lay hard against the wound on his leg. It was a bleeder. An artery had likely been affected. He was not going to make it, and neither Del nor I could change that.

"What are they doing on the tracks up here?" I repeated.

Hank didn't respond, his gaze shifting toward his already dead comrades.

"Why did he put them along the track?!" I shouted.

The dying man looked up, almost quizzically, as if he was offering up the obvious.

"For the cleanse."

The cleanse...

We'd heard that from the women we'd encountered in Whitefish. Rumor there, now it seemed to be confirmed. But just what was it?

"What is the cleanse?" Del asked, lowering his rifle now.

Hank drew a long breath. His gaze swam as he looked up to us and smiled.

"It's going to make everything better," Hank said. "Purify the land. Sterilize it, Major Layton says. Then things will grow...will grow again."

Some of what Hank was relating began to fill in a new picture. One beyond baiting Del and me into the open. Far beyond.

"What do those cars hold?" I asked.

"Some chemical," Hank answered, coughing again, one of his hands slipping from its place on the leg wound, his strength fading fast. "Flammable. Really supposed to burn, Major Layton says. When the wind's right he's gonna...he's gonna..."

The man's eyes fluttered and he looked off to one side, into the grey trees marching down the slope toward a rushing creek. Snow melt from the peaks had fed it, the tiny tributary raging now, soft roar rising.

"Gotta get to the bunker..." Hank said, the statement born of delirium. "He's gonna blow 'em up. Start the cleanse. Gotta get to the bunker."

"Is that where the Major is going to ride out this cleanse?" I asked, crouching and reaching to turn hank's face toward mine. "In this bunker he has people building?"

Hank nodded drowsily, smiling.

"We're all going to see the world when it's green again," he said, and then he said no more, his cheek tipping solidly against my hand where it lay against his head.

"Son of a bitch," Del said, shaking his head. "Sterilize? More like incinerate."

I pulled my hand back and Hank's head lolled against his shoulder as I stood. Behind, the damage we'd done to Major Layton's force was apparent. The men he'd sent were dead. Five in the blast and immediate follow up gunfire. And then there was Hank. Number six.

"When summer hits and he gets his winds," Del said, needing to add no more.

"Half the state will burn," I said.

"Including us."

Thirty Three

"Is this working?"

It was more plea than question that I watched on the television, the Denver station broadcasting again, though the face staring into the camera was no professional anchor. The woman was disheveled. Thin, but not emaciated. Her eyes were clear and wide, gaze darting off camera every few seconds toward some unseen other talking to her.

"Can they hear?"

I thought I heard someone in the background say faintly *'pick that up'*. A second later the woman had a small microphone laying atop the anchor desk in hand. She held it close to her mouth, just below her chin.

"My name is Jennifer. There are seven of us today." She paused and looked past the camera again. Behind her, the monitors that had once showed the red rectangles infecting other stations were blank and dark, powered down, as was most of the working studio visible over her shoulder, just a few errant overhead fluorescents flickering. "How do we know this is doing anything?"

Someone behind the camera seemed to say *'We don't. Get on with it.'*

Jennifer nodded and made sure the microphone was in place.

"There are seven of us," she started again. "A week ago there were nine. We're trying to make it, but we don't know where Eagle One is."

Eagle One...

"You have to tell us," Jennifer pleaded. "If you can hear this, or see this, tell us where you are."

I noticed then that something lay on the desk in front of her. Where an anchor might place notes, or a script of the broadcast in case the teleprompter failed. It was a single sheet of paper, rumpled, and it had not been there when I watched the man walk off camera, the last moments of life spilling from his wrist. Every few seconds, as she continued to beg for this enigmatic Eagle One to provide them with more information, the hand not holding the microphone would pinch at the edge of the creased paper, nervously, either some tic, or some more profound hesitation.

'Now. Do it,' the unseen party to the broadcast urged.

Jennifer looked past the camera and nodded, her gaze then dipping to the paper that had caught my attention. She hesitated, then lifted the paper so that it faced the camera.

"What the hell..."

It was all I could do to dial back my reaction and avoid some more vulgar profanity as punctuation.

"This is what we can bring," Jennifer said, then glanced down at what she held.

It was not just some piece of paper bearing writing, as I had supposed without seeing it. It was a photograph, in stark color, of a man's chest opened up, surgical instruments and wires holding the skin back and keeping the ribs spread, revealing a glistening heart, presumably beating. Blue-gloved hands were just visible in the image. A doctor. No, a surgeon. Some sick specialist who had opened up a living, breathing person for...

For what? What the hell did this mean? Who was the person in the photo? Who were Jennifer and her unseen companion?

And what the hell was this Eagle One thing?

"Tell us where to come," Jennifer said, thrusting the picture forward, closer to the camera, so that it blocked most of her face.

The transmission began to falter.

'We're losing power!' the warning came from off camera.

Static began to drizzle over the image like snow.

"Please," Jennifer said past the gruesome image.

I stared at the open chest and the bloody muscle within as the picture turned fully to electronic noise.

* * *

"That's...disturbing," Del said.

I'd left my house and walked to his, reaching it just after dark, sharing what I'd seen and heard on the Denver station.

"First you hear someone mention an Eagle One, and now I see this. It's not just an isolated coincidence."

Del nodded. He tipped his wrist and looked at his watch. The rugged old timepiece, with its manually wound mechanism, would probably be ticking when the two of us were worm food.

"What time did you see this?" Del asked.

"Had to be no more than an hour ago."

"That fits," he said, then read my quizzing expression and explained further. "I heard that same child broadcasting, and they signed off with the Eagle One thing. About two hours ago. I did a little direction finding by rotating the antenna. Signal was strongest when I was turned west."

"Two hours," I repeated, thinking. "Before the Denver people went on the air."

"Yeah," Del said. "And that picture you described, the one I called disturbing..."

"What about it?"

"In the transmission I heard, that kid read off a whole list of things. No context given, just one thing after another. But they were all medical related. Scalpels, IV tubes, stuff like that. And vascular clamps."

Vascular...

"That's for the heart, right?"

"If I remember correctly," Del said.

I stood and paced across Del's living room, shaking my head, beyond puzzled.

"Hey..."

I looked back to my friend.

"This is not our concern," he said. "We don't know what the hell it is, or even if it's anything. All we do know is it's a helluva long way from us. We have issues right here. And getting closer."

Closer?

"What's up?" I asked, walking back toward Del.

"Layton's men were talking back and forth about getting supplies ready for the outpost."

"What outpost?"

"Not sure. But they mentioned the highway where the firefight was."

"They said that?" I pressed. "They talked about the firefight?"

Del nodded. The only firefight they could have possibly referenced was the one I'd witnessed from a distance months ago. At a specific point on the map. One much closer to us than Whitefish.

"We need to put eyes on that spot," I said. "Was there any mention of a timeframe?"

"Yeah," Del answered. "Tomorrow."

Thirty Four

The column came up the highway and settled in the precise spot they'd mentioned on the radio, setting up what could only be described as some sort of forward observation post. We watched them from the wasting knot of fir trees two miles away, passing the binoculars between us, scanning their numbers, in groups gathered around one of their three vehicles and entering and exiting the tents they set up beside the highway. Each and every man was armed, though they seemed unconcerned with their immediate surroundings. The sentries they'd stationed at the perimeter of their camp were focused north. In our direction.

"Twenty," Del said, adjusting his body where he lay on the rocky ground. He grimaced quietly. The pain was worse today. Yesterday it was worse than the day before.

"I got the same count," I said. "That's a good portion of his forces."

He lowered the binoculars and nodded. When he'd first spotted this band near Whitefish a few hours earlier, they'd been offloading equipment from a larger truck. Now they were settling in, most certainly sent by Major Layton to seek out those who'd done continuing damage to his force.

"I get the sense these are not individuals of high moral character," he said, appraising the distant collection of men armed and ready to bring the fight to us. After a moment he sniffed a laugh. "I'll be damned."

"What?"

"The one in the blue coat, looking like he's leader of this squad...I recognize him."

"From where?"

"Your place," Del said, lowering the binoculars to look at me. "He's the guy who fired at me when they were raiding your barn."

"You sure?"

He lifted the binoculars again and confirmed his identification.

"I'm sure."

Again the binoculars came to me and I zeroed in on the man Del had described.

"Shoulda put a bullet in him," Del said, to himself mostly. "But you kill when you need to, not just because you can." He quieted for a moment and glanced to his backpack lying on the ground next to him. "When you need to..."

The last words were mostly whisper, most definitely between Del and something within. Some deeper understanding.

"Stay here," Del said, and slipped into his backpack as he scooted back from the thinning copse of fir trees and stood.

"What are you doing?"

"Moving for an advantage," he said, then nodded toward my AR. "You be ready on that thing. Give me ninety minutes."

"You want to fill me in on the plan?"

"You'll know what to do when the time comes," Del assured me, smiling as he slung his bolt action and headed off down the back slope of the rise.

I puzzled at the quickness of his departure, and the cryptic manner in which he was executing some action, wondering what benefit there would be to keeping me in the dark until...

...it happened.

A sickly feeling swelled instantly within and I looked behind into the grey woods, but Del was already gone.

No, I told myself. No way he would do *that*. But still the worry nagged at me, and continued to as I waited. I'd expected it to take the ninety minutes Del had asked for, but that time passed, and then two hours. Finally, nearly two hours and fifteen minutes after I'd last seen my friend, I glassed the scene in the distance, movement in a gully to the west of the outpost alerting me that Del had finally neared them.

"What the hell are you doing, Del?"

I had no answer as I watched him creep closer along the shallow depression, the whole thing playing out in an eerie silence, like a movie robbed of the texture that was sound. He drew within twenty feet of their position before I noticed something.

He didn't have his rifle. Not slung, and not in hand. Just the backpack strapped to his shoulders.

"Shit..."

I uttered the word even before seeing what he did next. He stood and stepped from the cover of the gully, approaching the group casually. They sprang into action, bringing weapons to bear, all aimed at Del, his own hands held upward. Demonstrating that he was no threat.

I suspected there was little truth in the gesture.

They motioned him closer, then down to his knees. The group huddled close, a pair of younger men stepping closer still, one reaching to Del's pack, still strapped to his back. Fingers gripped the zipper and pulled it to reveal the contents.

That was when I saw the flash. A bright white pulse erupted around Del and those who had subdued him, a dusty halo of dirty brown bursting outward an instant after that, billowing upward, some mini-mushroom cloud rising.

The sound reached me next, a sharp *BANG* and fleeting rumble, the sound echoing across the valley, bouncing off hill and mountain, until it was gone. Like my friend.

I lowered the binoculars for a moment, not wanting to see what lay there as the smoke and dust cleared. But I had to look. I had to see what Del had accomplished. Had to know if the sacrifice he'd crafted in secret had played out as intended.

What I saw would have made him smile.

Twenty men had come from Whitefish to hunt us down. Through the thinning smoke I now saw only two that moved, both on the ground, one writhing, the other furiously working some handheld radio. The rest either lay still alone or heaped together, or in pieces strewn about surrounded by red streaks upon the ground.

I could see nothing of my friend. He was simply gone.

Thirty Five

The door was unlocked. I entered and stood in the quiet for a moment. A quiet I'd become accustomed to since the hum of refrigerators and the whir of a vacuum motors ceased, along with virtually all who had enjoyed their convenience. Even in a strange place the quiet welcomed me. Soothed me. Surrounded me as I mourned.

Forty years Del had lived in the simple, comfortable cabin. A few rooms. Out back, a work shed. An equipment barn. About the only thing even remotely modern in the whole place was his amateur radio setup. He was a proud Ham. Or, as he'd called himself, a *voyeur of the airwaves*.

I turned the radio equipment on. The frequency was dialed into the one on which Major Layton's orders had been broadcast from Whitefish. That very station was transmitting, the operator seething, some auditory equivalent to foaming at the mouth.

"You will be hunted down, and you will be killed! All of you! Anyone who aided, or knew, or even laid eyes on the terrorist who attacked our protective patrol today will pay with your life!"

The threat continued. I listened, and I began to smile. Del would be enjoying this immensely. His selfless act had hit the Major, and hit him hard. I wished that it was the man himself unleashing the tirade, but I had no way of knowing.

That wasn't quite correct, I told myself, eyeing the handheld radio in its charger next to Del's base station. I picked up the radio and turned it on. Del had it set to some frequency distant from that which Layton was favoring. The small speaker spat silence, and silence only. Next to the volume knob was the squelch control, setting a limit on how much static would be heard, leaving the channel quiet until a signal strong enough came over the airwaves. I adjusted the squelch down and the grating static leapt from the speaker.

Adjusting the frequency and pressing the transmit button on the side of the radio with my thumb would take no effort at all. I could call out to Layton. From right here. Just as I could from the base station. I could let him know that what Del had done was only the beginning.

But that would be a mistake. There was every possibility that the signal would lead them right to me. That was an unnecessary risk.

Still, Layton needed to hear from me. And he would.

* * *

"I want to talk to Layton," I said, holding the transmit button on the handheld down.

Silence was the response I received. I checked that I had set the correct frequency and shifted my position, to the full crest of the hill now, one of the tank cars visible below, the last one in line and closest to Whitefish. The town itself was mostly dark, just a few open fires visible across dim distance, and, maybe, a splash of artificial light filling the windows of some building. Some important building on generator power. We were nearing the point where stored gasoline and diesel would be losing its ability to reliably combust, putting the usage of generators, and vehicles, and locomotives potentially on shaky footing. I imagined Major Layton knew this as well. He wouldn't be able to send patrols as far as he had attempted. Wouldn't be able to move tank cars around to place them for maximum effect. His plan to cleanse the land would, presumably, require the expenditure of fuel. Using locomotives to shuttle tank cars east, west, and south. Vehicles would have to bring men to set charges to blow the chemicals within the steel cylinders. He was going to wait for summer winds, as his man had shared, but he couldn't wait too long.

"Major Layton, are you out there? I can hear your broadcasts. You should be able to hear mine."

The half-moon drizzled weak light over the dead landscape. It was still odd to not hear an owl hoot, or a coyote howl. The nights were quiet. As quiet as the day.

I didn't have to suffer the silence very long.

"This is Major Layton."

The voice came clear over the radio. Strong, confident, collected. This was not the person who'd spat the threats earlier. This was a leader.

I had to remind myself that he was also a monster.

"Hello, Major."

"Who am I communicating with?"

I'd already decided how I would answer this question if asked.

"Me? I'm the man who's going to end you."

"That's a fairly arrogant pronouncement."

"Call it what you want," I said. "Call me what you want. Tell what's left of the world I'm a terrorist like your lackey on the radio earlier. The end will be the same—you're going to die."

The frequency was quiet for a moment. I could imagine Layton on the other end, smirking at my bravado, conferring with associates, maybe attempting to determine where my signal was coming from.

"It seems to me that you should be the one who worries about being taken out," Layton said after the silence. "The numbers aren't in your favor."

"They're less in your favor after the damage we did to your men."

"I'm far from being out of troops. While you, well, one of yours had to blow himself up to take my people out. Wouldn't that make this 'we' you mentioned a 'you' now?"

He was still playing cool. In the distance I saw vehicle lights come on. Two, three, four, the convoy speeding away from a single point downtown. Roaring west toward the highway.

They were onto me. My signal had given me away.

"Enjoy the time you have left, Layton," I said, taking the last word for myself before switching my radio off.

Nearly eight miles I'd traveled from my refuge to put distance from it and the signal. A three hour walk lay ahead of me as I headed home.

I could not have guessed what I would find waiting for me there.

Thirty Six

It leaned against my front door, butt on the floor of the porch, muzzle touching the old wood slab next to the lock.

"Del..."

I hadn't returned home since witnessing his sacrifice, having gone straight to his house, then off to speak my piece to Layton over the radio. Standing at my house finally, I understood why the ninety minutes Del had requested me to wait had extended beyond two hours. He'd hustled back here to leave me his rifle before setting off on his last trek. His last act.

The simple bolt action wasn't much to look at, weathered, scratched, its scope twenty years old and showing wear on the lenses. I climbed onto the porch and picked it up. The old weapon felt heavy in my hands. Much heavier than its mere weight. It bore the spirit of the man who'd carried it. The man who wanted me to have it.

But it was not just a gift Del Drake had left me. I believed he was speaking to me with the gesture. He was telling me not to continue the fight—he was telling me to finish it. In as much as I'd voiced my intent to bring an end to Major James Layton, Del, my friend, was simply reinforcing what, I suspected, he already knew I would do. The rifle was his vote of confidence in me. His blessing of me as a good man unwilling to simply do nothing.

The truth, though, as whole as my intent was, the how of my promise had not coalesced. For certain I could wage a one man guerilla campaign against Layton and his men, picking them off by ones and twos. In that scenario I would likely be taken out before ever getting near the man. To get to him I'd have to get through the others.

Or take them all out at the same time.

I looked to Del's rifle. He'd left his weapon of choice behind in favor of a way to do maximum damage. Could I do the same?

There would be no sneaking into Whitefish as some human bomb like my friend. We...*I* had four sticks of TNT left. Not enough to level a town.

Or was it?

Maybe, I thought, if it had some help. It could work, I told myself. I could *make* it work. There were pieces to put in place, but nothing seemed insurmountable. Even the way to initiate it I could manage. I slipped my small pack off and took the handheld radio from it, switching it on. Layton's man was haranguing the world and me specifically over the airwaves again. Turning it off would quiet the annoyance, but, instead, I turned the squelch up until the signal was not strong enough and the speaker quieted. Then I adjusted it down a hair and the screaming man was back. Up slightly, and he was gone.

I smiled and turned the radio off, hiking back to Del's immediately to retrieve the other handheld and chargers for both. When I returned I set about testing what I hoped would work, disconnecting the wires powering the speaker on one of the radios and connecting the leads to a bright LED flashlight bulb. Outside, I leaned the ladder against the barn wall and climbed to the roof, placing the modified handheld at the peak before switching it on and turning the squelch down fully. Had the speaker still been in place, crisp static would be sounding, but, instead, the power meant to construct sound from the device now set the bright and tiny bulb to shining. Setting the squelch near its maximum, the light went out. From my belt I took the unmodified radio and tapped the transmit button quickly, sending a quick, voiceless transmission. Set to the same frequency, the modified radio received the strong signal and the light flashed on for an instant.

"Right," I said, and climbed down from the barn roof, leaving the modified radio there and returning its near twin to my pack. It was time for the real test.

In the dark I hiked to a rise nearly five miles from my refuge, peak of the mountain rising another two thousand feet from the spot I'd set out for. It was familiar. I'd camped there before on hunts, the appeal of the level area its elevation for observation, and the more personal fact that, from it, I could look directly across the forest to my refuge. The line of sight was perfect, and I needed to do no more than bring the binoculars to my eyes and tap the transmit button one more time so that, across the distance, I could see the light affixed to the radio blaze bright atop my barn.

I turned off the radio and sat for a moment on a cool rock bulging from the earth. I had my detonator. Now all I needed was a bomb big enough to turn Whitefish to rubble and bring the very cleanse that Layton envisioned right to his doorstep.

In the morning, I thought to myself. I'd work then on securing the part that would go *boom*.

Thirty Seven

It sat where I remembered, weathered by winter and drenched through the early tantrums of spring. Ten years old, it had to be, the white body work showing patches of sanded rust, logo of the Federal Railway Administration faded on each door. The ungainly small metal wheels inboard of its standard tires seemed out of place where they hung beneath the frame. I'd seen the vehicle, and others like it over the years, driving normally along a roadway, then swinging onto a set of train tracks and lowering the secondary set of wheels, the combination of rubber and steel allowing the old but powerful Chevy to speed along rails meant for behemoths ten times its size.

Porter...

Ed Porter. That was the man's name. The one who lived out of the way in Stryker, a blip on the map that made Fortine look like Missoula, and Eureka like Las Vegas. He was an inspector for the Railway Administration, or had been. I'd run into him once on a hunt, and shared a conversation over some fresh venison backstrap. His job, as he'd explained it, consisted mostly of tooling up and down the tracks between his home base and Missoula, verifying that the private operators were living up to their commitments to keep the line safe and maintained. All he had to do, as he put it, was avoid being on the track at the same time as some thousand ton monster fully able to obliterate him.

And this was his ride. Parked just outside his small house a few hundred feet from the siding off the main track. A three hour walk through the grey woods had brought me here. I looked through the window and saw the keys in the cup holder hanging from the heater vent, but I didn't open the most certainly unlocked driver's door. Not yet. I had something else to do first. Inside.

I turned to Ed's house, white paint peeling in places. New shingles stark like islands surrounded by old roofing, some personal repair handiwork evident. Hesitation stalled me from mounting the front steps. What I might find inside held me back momentarily. But the horror of Ed Porter in death was not all that stalled me.

I was tired. Exhausted. Not from mere physical exertion. It was beyond that. It was almost...spiritual. Inside I felt increasingly hollow, the emptiness deepening with each step I took away from the man I'd been and toward the person I needed to be.

Or was choosing to be.

I had killed. More than once. And now I was going to kill again, without any moral argument against what I'd planned coming to mind. It was that far I'd come. How much I'd changed. On the hike from my refuge to Stryker I wondered on that, and on just how many degrees difference there were between what Major Layton was, and what I was becoming. He killed. I killed. There was the point of motive to consider. I knew that. But the end result, an acceptance of killing as a necessity, seemed hardly distinct at all. People were going to die at my hand, the Major among them, hopefully, and I was okay with that.

In fact, I was looking forward to it. To an end. An end of something. Something that I could control. Me. The wider world had spun itself toward self-annihilation. A microbe had found the genetics of the planet's flora irresistible. All things had brought me here, to Stryker, to

Ed Porter's house. And from here I would do the thing I had chosen to do, not that had been chosen for me.

Anarchy had settled upon the world, from continent to continent, in every corner. True enough. But I was my own order.

I mounted the steps and forced the front door open, its simple latch snapping the door jamb as I put my weight against it. No stench filled the space even though I could see the body in the easy chair, head tipped back, skin pulled taut over bone, mouth gaping open in death. The room was cold, nearly ice cold, the full spring warm up still to come. What had to be the remains of Ed Porter had been preserved, almost mummified in the dry environment within. That would not last, I knew. In days, maybe, the decay would begin in earnest, and what was left of the man I'd once shared a wild meal with would be set upon by maggots and flies. They survived, of course. Thrived, even, as one by one those of use who'd swatted and sprayed them dropped dead. Circle of life in all its gory glory.

I turned my attention away from Ed, who, during our feasting on venison had regaled me about trains. Anything and everything trains. In the garage out back of his house, if I cared to look, I might find the model railway setup he had described. The weather had been held at bay by windows that remained unbroken, and on his walls, undisturbed, were picture after picture of trains, locomotives and the cars they pulled, most, if not all, taken by Ed himself during his travel up and down the rails.

And, in a wall unit to the left of his fireplace, books. And books. And more books. Every last one about some facet of trains or railroading. There were generic books, resplendent with beautiful photographs of engines, old and new. Novels where the setting was aboard a train. And technical manuals on everything from vintage steam locomotives to the proper maintenance of switching equipment. Among the latter I found what I'd hoped would be here, a binder than had to be thirty years old titled '*Brake Testing And Service Under Adverse Rail Conditions*'. I could imagine Ed snapping up the obscure manual in some used book store, giddy with delight at his discovery.

I took the book from its place on a low shelf and flipped through it, pages and pages of yellowed diagrams and instructions nearly overwhelming me. But only until I found what I thought I needed. A simple schematic, actually, addressing the steps to take in releasing frozen brakes on rolling stock. Like box cars and tank cars.

I pulled the page from the manual and, carefully, slipped it back in place, the gesture of maintaining the sense of cleanliness and order Ed Porter had held himself to almost natural. A decent man sat behind me, dead. If possible I suspected Ed would have chosen to die on the rails. Maybe at the controls of a locomotive. But here, surrounded by reminders of that life he loved, was as close as he could get. And I wasn't going to sully what he'd made for himself.

"Rest in peace, Ed," I said, tucking the paper I'd taken into my pocket and heading out.

My next challenge, no less important than what I'd just found, sat before me. The truck. I opened the door and reached to the cup holder without getting in, slipping the key I retrieved into the ignition and rotating it forward. The response I got was a disappointing click.

The battery was dead.

A winter in the cold, without use, made it not surprising at all that I wouldn't get the engine to crank. Not on the first try. And not with that battery. I'd expected as much.

The garage sat just behind the house, wide barn type doors closing off from outside. I pulled one half open and took a small flashlight from my pocket to light up the space. The elaborate train table dominated the garage, stretching almost fully across the width, maybe a foot on the left side, and two on the right, just barely enough room to pass. I side stepped along the wall with more clearance and emerged at the back of the space, more traditional contents here. An axe. Shovel. Gas can.

And a spare battery.

I adjusted my AR to hang fully behind my shoulders and crouched, picking the battery up, cradling it in front as I began to shimmy along the train table, making it half way when the garage door slammed shut and the whole structure seemed to tip, wall behind slamming into me. The battery tumbled from my grip and onto the train table, crushing a station in miniature that had been expertly crafted. I fell forward with it as the table collapsed. Above, the open rafters shook, and items that had been stored in the recesses below the roof began to rain down, boxes of Christmas lights and childhood toys crashing and shattering. I groped for a handhold to steady myself and scrambled across the broken table as the wall I'd just stood against splintered and a massive brown paw punched through, long black claws stretched wide, reaching out.

"Shit!

I rolled and grabbed my AR from behind, swinging it toward the paw as it pulled back, claws grabbing at the exposed clapboard siding, a two foot chunk disappearing as it was ripped out, blinding bolt of sunlight slanting through as I fired, four rounds spitting out of the suppressor.

The wild beast screamed outside, a guttural cry, not of defeat, but rage. Within a few seconds it charged back at the garage wall, head and one paw tearing through. The mighty creature, usually muscled and stout, poked through gaunt, patches of its chestnut fur missing. It had surely awakened from its winter slumber in the past two months to find the world changed. To find the food it craved gone. Had it found others of its kind during this new famine it faced and feasted upon them? Is that how it had survived until now when it saw me as, possibly, its last, best hope for further survival?

It was a fighter. But so was I.

I took fast aim, ignoring the view through the tactical scope, and fired straight at the bear's wide face, four shots, each connecting. At least one appeared to traverse the nasal cavity and penetrate the wasting male's brain, as the near quarter ton bear went almost instantly limp, head and paw caught in the opening it had punched, the rest of its body falling slack outside. A last, steamy breath slipped from the grizzly, and then no more.

All that had tensed about me relaxed at once, the sensation one of instantaneous and total exhaustion, strength and determination draining away. For nearly half an hour I sat on the remnants of the mangled train table, back against piled boxes that had fallen from the rafters. I could have slept, but I didn't let myself. My brain and my body simply existed there for a time, not thinking or moving, the dead grizzly before me. Finally I made myself rise and put a hand to the bear's head, stroking his coarse fur. He'd only been doing what was in his nature to survive. As was I.

I gathered the battery from where I'd dropped it and carried it out of the garage. It slipped into the spot vacated by the dead battery and the truck turned over after gasping a few times. The gauge read only a quarter tank, and though it might not take that much fuel to accomplish what I needed the truck for, I topped it off once I reached my refuge, using the covert driveway at the north end of my property.

For the first time in a while a pickup sat between my house and the barn. The pieces were mostly in place. But, like Layton, I had to wait.

For the wind.

Thirty Eight

Three days into summer it came.

Spring had fizzled, dry and bleak. The blight had taken not only what there was, but what might have been. That was what spring was to me—a time of possibilities. In the mountains, the valleys, the cities and towns, winter slumber was pushed aside for life to flourish. Old and new. It was the clichéd time of beginnings. Three months of birth and rebirth. Once, it had been that. Now it simply passed as a date on the calendar and the sensation that the warm-up had come.

And with it the wind.

I had no idea the exact conditions Layton was waiting for. There were no vast meteorological services to inform as to whether a wind event was to be short lived, or sustained. But, if the dying man was to be believed, Layton had grown up in Whitefish. He would very likely be operating on memory. An ingrained sense of when the wind he wanted was more than transitory. I couldn't wait that long. I had only one condition.

It had to be blowing furiously from the north.

An almost nostalgic blast from what winter had been, the wind came, cool and dry, slipping beneath a sky of deep blue and over the moonscape the earth had become. It started before sunrise and grew stronger, whipping steadily at thirty miles per hour, with gusts that had to top fifty on a few occasions. I suspected that Layton was going to wait. As yet, I'd found no preparation of the tank cars parked along the rail line during my times patrolling. There'd been no sign of any push north from Whitefish. Layton and his men, it seemed, had decided to avoid confrontation and prepare for the cleanse.

I could wait no more.

I loaded what I needed into the back of Ed Porter's truck, the more delicate gear on the passenger seat to ride next to me. Before leaving I paused and looked back at my house, my refuge. The odds of me returning were beyond my ability to calculate. What I was about to attempt would either work, or not. One possibility in the latter aspect of failure could very well be the end of both me and the place I'd called home for more than half a year.

Neil was gone. Del was gone. If that was my fate by the time the day was up, I would join the many and leave the few. I only hoped I could take Layton with me.

I climbed into Ed's truck and drove down the hidden back driveway, turning onto Weiland Road, reaching the main north-south highway a few minutes later, the tops of a few of the tank cars visible to the left as I headed south, nearing my destination just before noon. I steered onto the road grade crossing over the tracks, but did not continue. Instead I turned right, onto the tracks, positioning the vehicle over the rails where they transitioned over the asphalt crossing. Putting into motion what I'd practiced, I engaged the small rail wheels, hydraulics lowering them so that they settled onto the steel rails, taking the weight of the vehicle. Trying forward and reverse, the pickup moved as expected, and I set off down the tracks, south, in the direction of Whitefish.

There was a stop to make first. A stop that had to be made. Blocking the way to Whitefish was the last tank car, the one closest to town. I pulled up to it, bumper of the pickup just nudging the car's knuckle that would connect it to other rolling stock. I climbed out, taking the modified radio with me, LED light gone, just the bare speaker wires and extensions protruding from the plastic body. From the back of the truck I grabbed the small satchel we'd kept our scavenged TNT in. The explosives were already prepared with blasting caps and electrically operated fuses. I attached the package to the underside of the tank car and wired the modified radio to it, but left the power off.

Next I found the braking mechanism, and the connecting lines that would hook it to a longer train of cars. I severed the hoses and manually disengaged the wheel brakes. On the flat here, the tank car shifted just a foot or so, but did not start rolling on its own. That would take some help.

Ducking under the long brown cylinder, I turned the squelch on the radio almost to maximum and drew a breath as I turned it on. It held, stable, the TNT package—and me—still in one piece. I hustled to the pickup and eased forward against the knuckle again. The pickup's thick raised bumper creaked backward, bending, but holding as I gave the vehicle more gas, the tank car ahead moving now, ever so slowly at first. Then, as we transitioned onto a slight grade, the speed picked up. Soon I had the tank car moving at five miles an hour, then ten, then slowing again on a level stretch of track a few miles from town.

This was my stop. I opened the door and dropped my backpack and rifle as the pickup and tank car trundled forward. Both thudded almost gently down the berm that sat beneath the tracks and came to rest on soft earth. From the seat next to me I took a length of metal that I'd fashioned and fixed one end under the steering wheel and wedged the other against the accelerator pedal, forcing it all the way to the floor. The engine raced, pushing the tank car toward another downhill section of track. I had to go now.

I half-stepped, half-leapt from Ed Porter's pickup, landing awkwardly on the side of the berm, rolling to the bottom, the earth there rocky, one sharp slab of stone jabbing into my shoulder. It took me a moment to shake off the pain and grab a few breaths, but I had no time to spare beyond that. The gravelly berm slipped under my feet as I ran back up along the track. My pack and rifle lay a few feet apart. I gathered them up and looked south along the track to see the pickup and tank car accelerating down the grade ahead.

* * *

A quarter mile. That was the distance. Uphill. I ran it with my pack and suppressed AR in just under two minutes. At the top of the hill my lungs burned and my legs were shaking. Huge gulps of air did little to soothe the fire in my chest. Adrenalin pushed me beyond the gasping pain and I took the radio and binoculars from my pack, bringing the latter up to scan the town, focusing on the rail yard just east of the river. Tracking right, my view shifting west, I finally found the tank car, rolling at speed, Ed Porter's pickup pushing it. It was maybe thirty seconds from where I needed it to be. I had to be ready.

I removed the radio from my pack and turned it on, the flexible antenna atop it whipping in the stiff wind. With one hand on the radio, I kept the binoculars in the other, watching as the tank car crossed the rail bridge over the river, then passed the maintenance sheds. Finally it traveled under the Baker Avenue Bridge and reached a point in line with the train station.

"This is for you, Del," I said, then brought my thumb down on the transmit button.

Miles away the signal was strong enough to overcome the squelch setting, energizing the speaker wires and passing that charge along to the electric fusing. Tiny plugs of compressed accelerant ignited, jets of hot gas firing into the blasting caps, triggering miniature explosions that expanded into the sticks of TNT.

A painful whiteness filled the binoculars. My face turned half away as I dropped them, squinting at the bright bubble of misty gas expanding outward from where the tank car had been, the milky dome, hundreds of feet in diameter, igniting a second later, flashing into a yellow-orange fireball.

I felt the heat, painful, then the wash of scalding air, like the breathy roar of some dragon spat my way. The crack of the blast, louder than any thunder I could imagine, shook the ground and the ranks of dead trees behind me, knocking the dusty grey death from them, limbs snapping to litter the earth below. I forced myself to endure the searing heat and watched the wave of fire race across the train yard and into the city, coursing down streets like rivers of flame. Whole neighborhoods were swallowed by the conflagration in an instant, the blaze rolling over buildings, across the city, nearly to the woods at the south end of town. Licks of yellow and orange swept over the river and onto the crisp waters of the lake, reaching a hundred yards out past the shore before retracting like a misdirected breath.

It had to be mere seconds, but the consumption of Whitefish by the fire I'd sent played out in some sort of mental slow motion. The blasted remnants of buildings leveled by the explosion arced through the air trailing streaks of fire, settling almost gently to earth. The train station disappeared in a shower of hot orange and yellow, tentacles of flame reaching out, drawing ever closer to the high school, then across the field beyond.

Then, I could see no more with specificity. Whitefish simply burned, smoke rolling above the inferno, obscuring the horror until darkness came and the town was lit like a pyre, fire everywhere, a crematory turned inside out. Hell on earth unleashed.

By me.

Thirty Nine

I didn't pray for it, but rain came in the night, stopping the spread of the inferno beyond the southern edge of town, as if by divine providence. The cool water bathed me where I sat on the hill, watching the blaze consume street after street, buildings crumbling in upon themselves, gas tanks and vehicle tires adding miniature explosions in the midst of the maelstrom. Through the night I watched. When morning came I was still on the hill, awake, sleep impossible, the whole of the smoldering town before me too much to turn away from. As the clouds parted and the sun peeked through, I rose and began to walk toward Whitefish.

Bodies...

The first I saw bobbing on the river as I crossed the bridge and entered the eastern half of the town, just a charred form half landed on the muddy bank, arms and legs splayed like a skydiver in freefall. A few licks of flame still rose from a skim of the chemical that had poured into the waterway. Three more I saw in the middle of one street, where the façade of one building had collapsed and lay in mounds of shattered bricks. Perhaps they'd taken refuge in the masonry structure, believing it impervious to the fire. Likely the timber roof structure bursting into flame had convinced them of their mistake, but not soon enough that they might flee with their lives. As it was they lay in close proximity to one another, scorched rifles still in the grip of two of them. Fighters to the end.

Most of the remains I came across as I worked my way further east were alone. Individuals cut down by smoke and heat mid stride in the center of some side street, or appearing only as an appendage poking from still smoldering rubble. The crackle of wood embers bursting was the only sound beneath the stilled breeze.

Until I reached the bank.

The walls of the building had tilted in, crushing the entryway, metal frame mashed, glass door obliterated, stream of smoke pouring out and angling skyward. Beyond it I heard thrashing and crashing. And moaning. Someone was in there, and they were trying to get out.

I stood fast in front of the consumed structure and held my AR at the ready. An exhausted calm steadied me. And cold determination commanded me to act as the man crawled from the bank and fell to his knees in the street, a few yards away, burned face angled up at me. Heat had split the skin of his face, which hung in blackened flaps from each cheek, cooked red flesh below, veins throbbing. His mouth opened as if to say something, swollen lips grotesquely quivering, soot expelled as he coughed, black, sludgy mucus draining from twin holes where his nose used to be.

"Hel..."

That was all he could get out. The 'p' eluded him.

I raised my AR and sighted past the suppressor at his chest.

All that is necessary for evil to triumph...

A steaming pistol was melted to a holster on his belt. He reached for it but fumbled with the weapon, bringing his hands up to see what the trouble was, his singed eyelids peeling back in horror as he saw that his fingers had been burned off, just blackened stubs of bone protruding.

The bank vault had obviously given him some protection. It had allowed him to live to see this moment. But no more.

I squeezed the trigger once and a *thewp* sounded. His body shuddered as the 5.56 millimeter round pierced his sternum. He tipped backward and fell into the gutter, blood spilling from the wound sizzling as it hit the superheated pavement.

I turned away from the man I'd just killed and looked east. The high school lay that way. There was more killing to do.

Five minutes it took me to reach what had been the town's high school. Just a smoking mound of stone, steel, and wood remained, stubborn pockets of flame having survived the early morning downpour to bubble hot and orange. I moved past the fallen structures, pausing to warm myself for a moment at one of the smallish fires. The wet cold of the night clung to me. The flickering little blaze did little to beat it back, leaving me tired and shivering, light wind swirling past, wicking still more of the scant warmth I had left. My knees softened without warning and my legs folded beneath me, sending me back against a heap of steaming rubble.

"I'm a good man," I said aloud, as if giving it voice might convince me enough of its truth to bring me to my feet again. "A good man."

I could not let myself do nothing.

I rolled to the side and used the butt of my AR to steady myself as I willed myself off the ground, looking past the remnants of the school to the field beyond, drifting curtains of smoke obscuring what lay there. What had to be there.

Layton...

When the tank car exploded and the wind dragged the raging fire into town, where would Major James Layton have gone? Where would he have retreated to?

To the very place he'd had constructed to ride out the inferno he was planning.

The smoke washed over me as I pushed forward, squinting at its acrid bite, shallow breaths burning until I emerged on the other side, the dirt field ahead charred, some boxy conglomeration of steel and concrete rising from what had once been the fifty yard line. Football players had collided there when chalk marked the once green turf. Fans cheered.

Now that spot was marked by the blackened hulk that Layton had made others build for him. How many had he allowed in with him when the fire, my fire, set upon them? Two? Ten? Twenty? Half buried in the poisoned earth, I guessed no more than ten could have fit in what I saw—if any had at all. Flames had reached it, leaping through the air on clouds of chemical vapor. Had the inferno choked the oxygen from the air within? Did the unbearable heat penetrate and turn those fortunate few inside to cinder? I didn't know. But I would.

I approached the bunker, mentally ticking off my place on the obliterated gridiron. Ten yard line. Twenty. Thirty.

That was when I saw the flash and felt the hot spear of copper and lead slice through my jaw, my body spinning as the crack of the first shot reached me. More followed, timed to impacts on the burned earth around me. Misses, my brain noted, the wound stunning me, slowing my reaction.

For a moment.

Stay alive...

Neil again, from memory, reminding me of the reason for my being, if not necessarily being here. I would stay alive. I would fight to stay alive.

I dropped to the ground and brought my AR into the fight, taking quick aim in the direction of the muzzle flashes still erupting from the side of the bunker and squeezing off a continuous stream of shots.

Distance is your friend. That was Del's belief. Here, though, I had to take the fight to those who were shooting at me.

The pain in my jaw almost inconsequential at that instant, I jumped up from the ground and, weapon shouldered for aimed fire, I advanced, continuing to pull the trigger in a rhythm set to the cadence of my movement—*shoot, step, shoot, step...* The quieted rounds spat from the suppressor and chewed at the stone and metal where the fire was originating. As I drew nearer, step by step, I began to see that I was being shot at not from within the bunker, but just outside, the attacker using its southwest corner for cover. I shifted my aim slightly and found a shape through the briskly drifting smoke. A form.

A person.

I fired four fast shots at the figure and they dropped, the final fire from their weapon, a single, wild round, slicing through the fabric of my coat, grazing the shoulder beneath. The fiery streak it dragged across my skin caused me to recoil, slowing me for an instant. But only an instant. Dropping the magazine from my AR, which was nearing empty, I inserted a full one and neared the corner.

A gaping square hole let into the bunker, hatch that covered it peeled back. Smoke drifted out, but no sound. Edging toward the corner I peered into the dark opening and saw little more than a single, large room, one tiny fire still burning within, wispy yellow light revealing a partly charred interior.

And a pile of bodies. Ten, maybe. Dead and alive, at least two showing some movement. Writhing in pain, hideously burned, the preparations to fully insulate the bunker incomplete. One side of the exterior showed partial progress in being covered by a layer of dirt, but the flames that had swept into town created a true firestorm, racing from building to building, leaping open space to penetrate the smallest opening. As it had here.

I ignored the interior and moved on, to the corner. Just around it I saw legs extending out, black boots at the end of each. A rifle lay next to them, an older G3, wood stock singed, a chunk of the receiver punctured and splayed open. At least one of my final rounds had rendered the weapon inoperable.

And the man who'd wielded it.

Major James Layton sat against the south wall of his bunker, choking smoke rolling past his blackened form. The left side of his body from chin to knee was seared, clothing melted to bubbled skin. Recognizing him was not difficult. He'd cut quite the appearance of authority the one time I'd glimpsed him through binoculars, greeting his train crew. Even with a portion of his face burned and the rest skimmed with sooty dust, I knew it was him.

His head rolled against the outside wall of the bunker and his eyes came up, settling on me.

"Goddamn murderer," he said.

I didn't respond to his words. For a moment I didn't say anything. I simply looked at him, up close, wanting to see, or sense, what might have been special about the man.

"Do you know what's truly pathetic about you," I said, my words stilted by the bleeding wound in my jaw.

Layton's swollen lips curled, to something I thought was a scoffing smile.

"You're a dime a dozen," I explained. "How many other guys are there like you who try stepping into an absence of order, to institute their own? Guys like you think power is leadership. You're a cheap wannabe dictator. Tell me, how is it you got out of your bunker while everyone else is pretty much burnt toast? Did you use them to protect you from the flames? If I checked, would I find bullet holes in some backs in there? Did you do that to make the uncooperative ones more amenable to being used as human shields?"

The strange grin he'd managed drained away, scowling animus rising in its place. I'd hit a nerve.

"I hope that hurts," Layton said, winking as he savored the sight of blood dribbling down my neck.

"Yeah, you got me. But I'm the one still standing."

Layton's expression went slack and he angled his face away.

"One more thing," I said.

He turned once again to look at me. When his gaze met mine I brought my AR up and put a single round through his forehead. A halo of red burst upon the dull concrete wall behind his head before it tipped forward, chin against his chest, back of his skull split open.

I wanted to look on him no more. Wanted to see this place no more. The urge to leave, to run, ran headlong into the reality of my situation. The finality of what had just transpired drew the numbing energy from my body and let the pain rush back in. I managed a few steps from the bunker before stumbling, my lower half settling limp to the ground in a lopsided half sit, stiff arm planted, keeping me partly erect like some anatomical kickstand.

A year ago...

That musing thought rose for some reason. The beginning of last summer. I was blissfully ignorant of the steamroller of change already creeping my way. Creeping the world's way. And I was happy. I was whole. I was clean.

Clean in a way I could never be again. Not after what I'd seen. What I'd done. Particularly what I'd done here. How many had I sent to their maker? How many deserved it?

All, I tried to tell myself. But that was Del talking, exhibiting the one flaw I could find in his character—a streak of moral absolutism. It was a trait both admirable and damning. He had been able to manage a life lived that way, maybe through the isolation he'd chosen for himself. No matter where he worked over the decades, he had his singular realm to retreat to. From him, because of him, I had found the will to do what I had.

I would be judged, I knew. But not there. Not then. With effort I returned to my feet and walked back through what had been Whitefish. I came upon no more survivors. I had done what I'd set out to.

Fourteen hours later I reached my refuge. With the last of my energy I cleaned the gunshot wound that had, from a quick examination, passed between my open lips and exited the back right of my jaw. I could barely open my mouth, spikes of agony erupting each time I tried. I wept as I swabbed the entrance wound inside my cheek with the strongest antiseptic I had. Wept and felt my head begin to swim. With shaky haste I caromed off walls and furniture and, fumbling my way down the hallway to my bedroom, tipped sideways onto my bed, blood soaking the pillow and mattress as I fell into a deep, dreamless sleep.

When I woke two days later I found a few sheets of paper and penned my last testament, no point in calling it a will. There was nothing to pass on, and no one to pass it on to. Somewhere in the rambling document I asked God for forgiveness. That night the sky turned black and stabbed at the earth with lightning and shook all around me with thunder.

It seemed to me I'd received the answer to the pardon I'd sought.

Forty

Summer came and went. I mashed food as I prepared it, slipping ever smaller bits past my lips. What I managed to swallow kept me alive. Barely.

Heat sizzled across the parched landscape. The winds that Layton had waited on ripped through the mountains. Dry lightning set patches of the matchstick woods ablaze across the valley. I watched smoke rise, a dark grey column climbing into the sky. For days I wondered if the wildfire might blow my way and visit upon me what I'd arranged for Whitefish, but soon the smoke tower laid down to the east as the flames were dragged that way by the winds. I was spared.

For the moment.

Every day I grew weaker. In the high heat of the season I found that I needed a fire even mid-day. My bones ached with a persistent chill. When I had the strength I cut wood. When I didn't I broke pieces of furniture. Once or twice a week I turned the television on and listened to the static where the Denver station had been.

The first week of September, the static went quiet and a darkness appeared on screen. Not total, some faint light hinting that I was still seeing the news studio. The chromed edges of the anchor desk gleamed weakly. One of the monitors mounted high on the wall beyond flickered slightly. It seemed empty as I stared at it.

It was not.

The figure slouched about in the near distance, weaving between desks in the working newsroom behind where the anchors once sat. Man or woman I could not tell in the dim space. They pulled drawers open and pawed at the contents, their form and actions lost in complete shadow more often than not. Still, I knew that they were there. I could hear them.

A microphone somewhere in the studio was picking up their movement. Their breathing. Even their voice. So thin and distant it was, though, that little could be determined from it. I turned the volume all the way up until the television speakers hummed, but all that did was make the unintelligible loud. Slipping from my place on the couch I slid across the floor until I was just inches from the screen, my hollowing eyes trying to peel through the darkness a thousand miles to the south.

The figure stepped from the full shadow and into some semblance of light. A wisp of it, at least. It was a man, I thought. Or at least the features of the head made me think so. And the voice now, it came through louder, closer to some microphone, the words breathy, but also sounding male beneath the vacant tone. And they were saying something I could just make out.

"I need my script."

The man staggered from the working newsroom to the anchor desk and tipped against it, single piece of white paper in one hand, the other grasping at the edge with fingers that were near skeletal. He leaned forward, face over the desk, more light angling upon him now, revealing his harsh features, skull chiseled down to thin skin draped upon bone. He was unrecognizable.

Except for the eyes.

"Jim," I said, and let my hand drift to the screen and lay upon the face of the veteran newsman.

"Thank you," Jim Winters began, swallowing dryly. "Thank you for joining us. In today's news..."

He hesitated, lost, eyes glancing down at the blank sheet of paper in his hand, an anger building, setting the blue in them afire as his gaze shifted, looking past the camera.

"Dammit, Mark! Why is the script not on the prompter?!"

The question, sharp and loud, was accompanied by a trickle of white froth at the corner of Jim's mouth, the bubbles soon turning pink, then red. A thin, dark trickle of blood dribbled from his nose and over his lips.

"Dammit!" he swore again, spitting the blood draining over and from his mouth, hand that held the paper bunching it into a fist that he slammed down upon the desk. "We need to be professional! People are counting on us!"

I drew my hand back from the sickening image on the screen as Jim Winters looked again into the camera.

"Ladies and gentlemen, I apologize for the difficulties we are experiencing. We will endeavor to...to..."

He quieted, his gaze drifting upward, to the darkness looming above.

"We need more light," Jim said. "More light and..."

Then he said no more. The fist he'd planted on the desktop opened, letting the paper slip out. He straightened with effort, standing behind the desk, running a hand over the few strands of hair that remained atop his head, grooming a memory. His body turned unsteadily, back to the camera, and he made his way back into the working newsroom, shadows swallowing him as he appeared to sit at a desk and let his head come to rest upon it.

I scooted away across the floor until my back was against the couch, watching for hours, past the time the sun disappeared in the west, my eyes tuned to the distant, dim studio, trying to seize on any movement. There was none. Not at nine o'clock. Not at midnight. And not at half past one in the morning when, once again, the Denver station went to static.

After a few minutes I turned the television off, muting the slight glow it had spread about the room around me. Night flooded in through the windows, dark and full. Out there, somewhere, I wanted to believe that there was hope. The hope that Neil had told me had to exist.

But I no longer thought that possible. The blight had wiped the world nearly clean of our kind, and we were fully capable of finishing what it couldn't. Hope was an illusion. Once it had been real. But no more.

I turned away from the television and faced the fire.

Stay alive...

Stay alive...

Neil's admonition haunted me as the fire spat embers.

Stay alive...

"I can't," I said, swollen and stiff jaw barely letting the two words out. "I can't."

Beyond that near certainty, I wasn't sure I wanted to.

As fall settled in, and the world remained grey, devoid of any brilliance nature had once allowed to soften the death that came with the season, I felt my energy and my body accelerate toward an end. I was ready to go, quietly, my flesh and spirit nearing the moment when they would begin to fade. The time to let the blight finally claim me was almost at hand.

Fate, though, crept forward on its own line of time, serving its own agenda. It was not done with me.

Forty One

I stared at death through the front window.

The pines stood like splintered matchsticks, poking from the dead brown earth. Where once stood a lush forest creeping toward green slopes and rocky peaks there now was a graveyard of mighty woods. My house, my safe place, was surrounded by a grey, silent end, that inevitability creeping closer to my own situation.

Eating had become torture, what I could get down coming up more often than not. Some infection, I suspected, had settled it. A parting gift from Major James Layton and the bullet of his that had found me. I'd exhausted my supply of antibiotics to keep any ill effects of the injury at bay. Now, I was at its mercy.

The last chirp of a bird or stomp of a rutting moose had long since faded. I hadn't seen a single living thing above ground since the random attack by a starving grizzly. Just the earthworms were left, I suspected, safe and waiting beneath those who had, somehow, stayed alive. And how appropriate was that? We all went back to worm food eventually.

Beep.

My head angled slowly toward the alarm panel. As long as the sun shined my security system would trundle on, giving false warnings. A branch falling and tripping a motion detector. A glint of reflected sunlight confusing a thermal sensor. Perhaps what I'd built here to alert for intrusions would offer up its beeps and buzzes in some manner of truncated perpetuity. Perhaps.

But I would not be here to notice. Or to care.

"If a tree falls in a forest," I muttered and tried to focus in on the alarm panel from across the great room. A fire roared in the hearth, no fear of marking my presence quelling the desire for heat anymore. I'd weighed myself that morning. The number that stared up at me from the old scale was a terrible truth. A hundred and seven pounds.

I'd topped out at one ninety the day the red signal had come.

Blankets wrapped me as I huddled near the blaze. Fall hinted hard at winter. Another winter. I couldn't shake the chill, light as it was. It seemed colder this year. Maybe it was, but I knew it was likely that my deteriorating physical state was responsible for the heightened discomfort. As it was for my fading eyesight. Straining to see across the room, I could hardly make out the boundaries of the rectangular alarm panel, even less so whichever specific warning had been tripped. It would reset in a minute, I knew. The sensor would realize that a fallen limb from one of the withered trees was responsible, the offending length of desiccated wood lying motionless on the ground. Moving no further through my secure perimeter.

Beep.

I turned back to the fire, staring into its shifting yellows and swirling oranges. On the hearth before it a charred pot rested. In it I'd cooked yesterday's meal, a mixture of rice and potato flakes. Calories, pure and simple. Taste didn't register anymore, and that which did was muted by the pain that registered in my wounded jaw with every small swallow. The joy that food once held, the pleasure, had long since left me, every morsel I consumed a reminder of what had brought me to this state of being. What had brought the world to its knees. Brought mankind to its end.

Beep.

Again I looked to the alarm panel, a small rectangular light pulsing, off and on, clear to red. The sensor had not reset, some electronic glitch preventing the alert from quieting.

Unless it wasn't a glitch.

Beep.

I planted my hands on the arms of the chair and pressed myself out of the seat, rising unsteadily, blankets shedding from my shoulders and mounding at my feet. A step took me just past the chair and I grabbed onto the edge of the mantle for support, logs spitting embers in the hearth as I passed. Another few steps brought me to the back of the couch. I gripped it with both hands like a railing and drew nearer to the alarm panel, still beeping, light flashing, close enough to see that it was an outer sensor that had tripped. One just inside my property line not near the driveway, but further into what had once been the deepest of woodlands, beyond the pond and stream, where the hills began to step toward mountains.

Beep. Beep.

A second alarm sounded, light flashing with it, nearer my house now. Closing in on me.

"I'm not checking out," I muttered to the empty space and grabbed Del's rifle where it leaned against the wall, nearly stumbling as I took control of the weapon. My friend's weapon. "Not walking into the fire. No way."

My thoughts tumbled about in a hazy waking state, recollections mixed with intention. The past with the here and now. Rendered images of a woman's suicide filtered through my tenuous consciousness. A pyre of flame, and me striding into it. Consumed.

Beep.

They were closer still.

"Distance is your friend," I said, borrowing my friend's tactical mantra.

The door lay just a few steps away. It twisted and warped in the grip of my mind's eye. What hold I had on the real was slipping. If I was going to confront the intruders, if I was going to make a stand, make a last stand, it had to be now.

I pushed off the wall with my free hand and aimed my body at the door. It tipped that way, feet shuffling to keep up as gravity pulled my upper half forward and down. Only the heft of the door absorbing the faint weight of what I'd become stopped me from toppling to the floor.

Another beep sounded behind. I cared no more where they were coming from, only that they were coming, and only that I would be waiting, ready, eager to see some end come. Hopefully to them before me.

I shifted to the right and planted myself against the wall, reaching to the door. With a breath and a guttural grunt I jerked it open. The cold inside was eclipsed by what washed in, whipping around me. With effort I brought Del's rifle up and worked the bolt, chambering a round as I stumbled forward, foot catching on the threshold, my body collapsing onto the porch's old floor boards. The impact punched the breath from me and left me gasping as I clawed my way toward the front steps.

The rifle bucked in my grip, just one hand holding it, finger squeezing the trigger as I lay atop the weapon. It thudded against my chest, then settled, and I rolled slightly off it to cycle the bolt again as I caught my breath.

"I'm ready for you," I tried to shout, but a voice hardly raised was all I could muster, the warning surely lost in the wind. "I'm taking you with me."

I fired again, not even bothering to aim. Little chance that I could have if I'd wanted to. My vision had degraded, through fatigue, malnourishment, or some internal malady, to the point that objects at any distance beyond a few yards seemed to be drifting beyond some gauzy veil.

"Keep coming," I challenged the intruder as I worked the bolt, and readied still another round.

Through the mental fog filling my head I wondered, though, why there was no return fire coming my way. No wood was splitting from the impacts of near misses. I had not been struck. There was no sharp report of shots cracking in the woods.

"Come on!" I yelled, the sound carrying this time, another shot following to punctuate my words.

But there was no assault in reply. No sound at all. Until...

Fletch...

The memory came from nowhere, Neil calling to me. Maybe I was already dead, I thought, in the place where my friend had been since succumbing in the early days of the world's slide toward the abyss.

Fletch...

Why he was calling to me I didn't know. I wanted to see him. To feel his presence again, even if only in some ethereal plane where souls gathered.

It's me...

I wanted to call out to my friend, but did not know how. In this other place, was I to just use my voice? Would he hear it?

"Stop shooting!"

The directive shook me from all consideration that I had transitioned to a place beyond this life. Those were actual words. Real words. Shouted at me. By...

No. It couldn't be. I was imagining it. Maybe the words had not been real. Maybe they were just part of my fading consciousness. Because that couldn't be...

"Neil?" I asked, as loud as I could. "Neil?"

"Yes!"

The answer came. From Neil. But was it him? How could it be him? This was some sick hallucination, I began to think, married atop a reality crashing toward me.

Someone out there wanted to kill me. Someone out there had breached my perimeter. It was not my friend. It was not Neil. My mind was playing tricks.

"No!"

I fired off another round, screaming as I did.

"Fletch, stop it! It's me!"

"It's not Neil! It can't be!"

I cycled the bolt again, but had exhausted the rounds in the internal magazine. It was empty. My mind seemed to ignore this point of certainty and I made some attempt to aim, rolling to line up my right eye behind the scope. The world beyond the glassy circle shifted like some funhouse mimic of what lay beyond.

"I'll kill you!" I threatened, and silence followed. My finger rested on the trigger. Waiting through five seconds, then ten seconds of thick, anxious quiet.

"Fletch!" the voice called out finally, then added, "Life's tough!"

Life's tough...

The voice out there had said that. I heard it. With my ears. It was not conjured by my mind.

Life's tough...

"You remember, Fletch! You have to remember!"

Life's tough...

"Be tougher," I mostly whispered to myself, then drew a great breath and shouted for all I was worth, right side of my face afire with pain. "Be tougher!" I pushed the rifle aside and grabbed at the porch railing above, trying to pull myself up, but only managing to get to my knees, hunched forward, like a worn warrior bent in prayer. "Neil!"

I tipped sideways, just above the steps, my head thudding off the cold wood, eyes fluttering open and closed, trying to seize upon the image of someone rushing toward me.

More than one someone.

"Neil..." I said, the word, the name, slipping out like some last gasp.

"Fletch! Fletch!"

It was him. It was Neil. Somehow, in some impossible way, my friend was here. And he was not alone.

"Fletch," he said almost softly as he reached me. "Shit."

Neil slipped an arm under my neck and lifted my head from the cold wood of the porch, cradling me. Beyond him I saw two more shapes. Hovering above. People. Women. One older, one younger. Mother and daughter? Were they real? Was he?

"You're alive?" I asked, and my friend nodded.

"So are you," Neil said.

I chuckled lightly, then my eyes closed, and I drifted off, toward dreams or death I had no idea.

Forty Two

"You're back," Neil said as my eyes opened and found him standing over me.

I was in my bed, in my refuge, the iron stove hissing hot, snow falling beyond the window.

"Neil...how..."

He eased himself to the edge of my bed and took my hand in his, squeezing hard to let me know I was really, actually alive.

"Plenty of time to hear my story," he said.

"Someone's awake."

It was the woman I'd seen with Neil as they came to me on the porch. I didn't see the girl, the child, now, and I wondered if that part of my hazy encounter had been a dream.

"Fletch, this is Grace," Neil said. "Grace, my friend Fletch. Eric. Eric Fletcher."

"I'll choose among your suggestions," Grace said, and knelt next to the bed, putting a hand to my cheek, her gentle touch muted by something—bandaging. "You're doing better, Eric."

I reached up and felt that side of my face. The sloppy bandage job I'd done after being shot by Layton had been replaced by something that felt somewhat competently done.

"Grace is a nurse," Neil told me. "She did the best she could with your ugly face."

"It wasn't too bad," Grace told me as she lifted an edge of the gauze to examine the wound. "You had some infection setting in, but we caught that before it turned septic. I stitched up the entry and exit wounds. You lost a molar, but mostly you're lucky that whoever shot you was off in their aim."

"Layton," I said, and Neil looked to Grace, both puzzling at the singular word I offered. "He shot me."

Neil nodded, some anger clear now on his face.

"I assume you gave better than you got," he said.

"Much," I replied. "How long have I been..."

Pain sizzled across the right side of my jaw, cutting off my question.

"You were out for two days," Neil told me. "Long enough for Grace to do her best work on you."

I looked between them, and then to the doorway, the hall empty beyond.

"When you came, I thought I saw a girl."

"My daughter," Grace said. "Krista. She's staring at the snow out the front window."

The trickle of data about me, Neil, Grace, her daughter, set my head to spinning, some hint of that externally obvious. Neil smiled at me.

"Don't sweat everything that's happening," he said. "We've gotta start getting food into you. Gotta get you stronger."

"I'm low on food," I managed to say.

"We came supplied," Neil said.

I wondered what the story was with Neil and Grace. They seemed infinitely comfortable with each other, yet I hadn't noticed even a slight expression of affection. No hand on his shoulder. No telling smile toward her. Maybe they had just met on the road, heading my way. Travelers of convenience. Or necessity. Safety in numbers.

"You're going to get better," Neil assured me. "You'll be ready."

"Ready?" I asked, my voice strained, hardly a dry whisper coming out. "For what?"

"To head west."

The voice was small and perfect. Grace turned toward it, her body shifting so that I could see Krista standing in the doorway, looking right at me with bright, hopeful surety.

"That's right," Neil said, looking to Grace now. "Right?"

Her face tightened, the smile that remained seeming strained now.

"Right?" Neil sought confirmation again.

Grace nodded, more acceptance than concurrence in the gesture.

"What's to the west?" I asked.

"Eagle One," Krista said from the doorway.

Eagle One...

Del had zeroed in on the signal he'd heard as coming from the west. I looked to Neil, the certainty about him pierced somewhat, if only by a degree. As if the journey that lay ahead was beyond necessary.

In fact, it turned out to be the only hope any of us had.

Thank You

I hope you enjoyed *Bugging Out*. Please look for other books in *The Bugging Out Series*.

About The Author

Noah Mann lives in the West and has been involved in personal survival and disaster preparedness for more than two decades. He has extensive training in firearms, as well as urban and wilderness Search & Rescue operations, including tracking and the application of technology in victim searches.